THE
STRETFORD
ENDERS AWAY

RED FOX DEFinitions

Also available in **DEFINITIONS**

The Stretford Enders by Trevor J. Colgan

Postcards from No Man's Land by Aidan Chambers

Dance on my Grave by Aidan Chambers

In the Money by Helen Dunmore

Going to Egypt by Helen Dunmore

The Tower Room by Adèle Geras

Watching the Roses by Adèle Geras

Amongst the Hidden by Margaret Haddix

Running out of Time by Margaret Haddix

They Do Things Differently There by Jan Mark

Love. in Cyberia by Chloë Rayban

Terminal Chic by Chloë Rayban

I Capture the Castle by Dodie Smith

The Leap by Jonathan Stroud

The Islanders by John Rowe Townsend

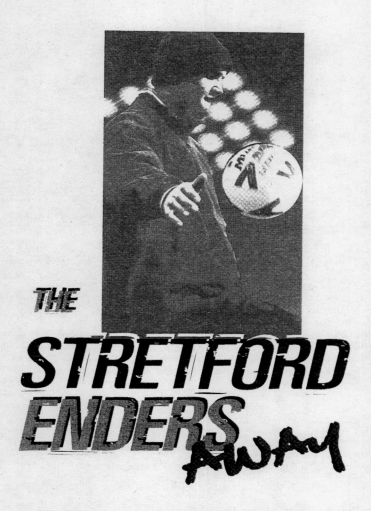

THE
STRETFORD
ENDERS AWAY

TREVOR J. COLGAN

RED FOX **DEfiNitiONS**

A Red Fox Book

Published by Random House Children's Books
61-63 Uxbridge Road, London W5 5SA

A division of The Random House Group Ltd
London Melbourne Sydney Auckland
Johannesburg and agencies throughout the world

First published in Great Britain
by Red Fox, 2001

Printed and bound in Great Britain by Clays Ltd, St Ives PLC

THE RANDOM HOUSE GROUP Limited Reg. No. 954009

ISBN 0 09 941704 9

www.kidsatrandomhouse.co.uk

contents

The Biggest Game of Luke's Life   1
The Stretford Enders vs. Stella Maris   9
End of Season Party   18
From Bad to Worse   33
Turnaround Has To Be Fair Play   51
Celebration   55
The Venue   59
One Last Chance   67
Face to Face with Weasel   74
The Start of a Long Hard Journey   82
Terry Culshaw's House   87
The First Trial Game   93
Disco Drowning Sorrows   99
The Second Day   114
Return of the Conquering Hero   120
Alone in the World   131
Trying Something New   137
Moving On   142
Five Days in Paradise   152
Setting People Straight   159
Battle Number Two   165
A Bed for the Night   168
Independence Day   172
Escape Plan   176
Making Your Way in the World   180
Getting Acquainted with Duncan   187
Waiting to Exhale   194
The Long Road Home   199
The Funeral   204
Keeping a Promise   209

For my son
Jack.

THE BIGGEST GAME OF LUKE'S LIFE

The final of the All-Ireland Under-Fifteen Schoolboy Cup was, without a shadow of doubt, the biggest game in the life of Luke Farrell and the history of the Stretford Enders. The game against Stella Maris was scheduled to kick off at 3pm in Tolka Park on Sunday, June 20th. It was now ten to two and Luke's mother, Martina Farrell, was nowhere to be seen.

'I don't believe this,' Luke said angrily. He paced the pavement frantically, staring up Montague Avenue towards the train station. He had been glued to the same spot for the last ten minutes, expecting to see a panicked Martina race round the corner from Main Street with an apologetic look on her face. But there was still no sign of her.

'Perhaps she's been delayed,' Ronald said.

Luke glanced down at Ronald, his mother's nerdy boyfriend from Holland, who sat behind the steering wheel of his orange Citroën. He felt like tutting loudly or splurting out some sarcastic reply. But Ronald wasn't to blame; he had arrived on time.

Luke turned his head slightly to look at Mrs Hendy, his and Martina's landlady and Luke's special friend, who sat in the back seat of the Citroën, directly behind Ronald. Although she did little more than smile and shrug her shoulders, Luke could sense the message in her calm blue eyes. 'Don't panic.'

Luke turned his attention back up the Avenue. As usual, Mrs Hendy had preached a piece of calm, rational advice. But Luke's pre-match nerves were dangling. He could feel the hairs on the back of his neck stand on end as his mind displayed a cruel flashback to the Templelogue Sports Ground, twelve months earlier. It had taken a lengthy explanation, two public apologies, six months of playful verbal abuse at training sessions and the nickname Lord Lucan to regain the complete trust of his team-mates.

If Luke were to miss a second consecutive Cup Final, he would have to think seriously about a transfer to another club.

A brown-haired woman turned the corner onto Montague Avenue. Luke dropped his jaw in anticipation. False alarm; it wasn't Martina.

'Arggh,' he groaned. 'She's doing this on purpose.'

Ronald opened the driver's door and climbed out to join Luke on the pavement. He glanced at his wristwatch before taking a speculative look up Montague Avenue. It wasn't like Martina to be late for anything. Luke and Ronald locked stares, both wearing expressions of anxiety and frustration.

'Five more minutes?' Luke said.

He expected Ronald to nod his head in agreement right away. But he didn't seem too keen on the proposed delay. He, of course, had first-hand experience of last year's Cup Final fiasco. Ronald had sat beside Luke in the Citroën last May as they battled their way unsuccessfully through Saturday after-noon traffic.

'I'll leave a message on her mobile,' Ronald said. 'She'll be sure to follow us.'

Luke watched Ronald climb back into the car. He under-stood his desire to prevent a second footballing disaster but was surprised by his willingness to abandon the wait for

Martina. Luke took one last look up Montague Avenue; still no sign of his mother.

'What a great start to the day,' he said quietly to himself before walking round to the passenger door.

Once inside the car, Luke pulled his seat belt across his chest while Ronald started the engine. Somehow he expected to sight Martina rushing onto Montague Avenue as they pulled away from the kerb, frantically waving her arms about to signal their halt. He kept a close eye on the people moving about Main Street as the car passed through Dun Laoghaire town centre. He gave eagle-eyed attention to the main entrance of the Bloomfield Shopping Centre as they rattled by, but there was still no sign of Martina.

'She'd better have a top-notch explanation,' Luke said.

Neither Ronald nor Mrs Hendy replied to his statement, which was delivered in a poisonous tone. In fact, this was the last remark made by anyone in the car on the journey to Tolka Park.

Despite a ten minute hold-up on a heavily congested O'Connell Street, Ronald, Luke and Mrs Hendy arrived safely at Tolka Park for half two. Ronald pulled the Citroën to a halt outside the entrance to the dressing rooms to allow Luke out first. He jumped out with his kit bag.

'Luke,' Mrs Hendy said. Luke ducked his head back inside the rolled-down window of the passenger door. Mrs Hendy smiled at him. 'For good luck,' she said softly. She held a silver medal in the palm of her hand. Luke smiled; he recognised it from the mantelpiece in the back parlour. It was Jimmy Hendy's winner's medal from the 1937 South Dublin Cup Final.

'Thanks Mrs H,' Luke said as he took her late husband's medal from her hand. He felt uncomfortable walking away from the car so soon after her noble gesture. But Mrs Hendy again employed one of her silent expressions, giving Luke the go-ahead to leave. He managed to get on to the pavement before Ronald called him back.

'Hey Luke, don't play so deep today. Remember, you lead the line.'

Luke nodded his head in agreement. Over the last twelve months he had come to realise that Ronald Van De Kieft knew a fair bit about football. He had attended all of the Stretford Enders' games that season, both home and away. And as a special fifteenth birthday present last June, Ronald had taken Luke and Martina over to Amsterdam to see Holland play France in the group stages of Euro 2000. Of course, he and Ronald just had to go back that September to witness the epic 2–2 draw between Holland and the Republic of Ireland in World Cup Qualifying Group Two.

'Hey, don't worry. She'll be here,' Ronald said.

Luke smiled. He nodded his head in agreement.

'Good Luck,' Ronald said with a smile. He rolled up the window and manoeuvred the car back on to the road. Luke waved at Mrs Hendy as they drove off to find a parking space.

The dressing rooms at Tolka Park were at the bottom of a dark tunnel beneath the main stand. Luke walked down the tunnel slowly, more interested in studying the inscription on Jimmy's medal than looking where he was going.

'Luke,' a voice said.

Luke turned round. Tonka Matthews, the Stretford Enders' enormous midfielder, stood at the door of the dressing room. He had shorts, socks and boots on, but no jersey.

'Is it him? Is it him?' Jerome asked anxiously from inside the dressing room. He nudged out past Tonka into the tunnel. 'Where've you been?' he yelled dramatically.

'Relax,' Luke replied coolly. He patted his manager on the arm before casually strolling past him and Tonka into the dressing room.

It was this laid-back gesture that lit the fuse. Jerome worked himself into a furious fit of rage. But he could find no action to articulate his anger. He paced about the tunnel, throwing his arms about theatrically. He tried to begin a rant, but all the words jumbled together and caused a blockage at the tip of his tongue. The only sound to escape his lips was a painful 'fff' or 'g-g-grrr'.

Jerome turned to Tonka for a show of empathy. And although the massive midfielder agreed Luke's attitude was dubious, he felt somewhat unnerved by the insanity in Jerome's wide white eyes. He was beginning to resemble an aggrieved Elmer Fudd or Yousamity Sam after a futile spat with Bugs.

Eventually, the verbal blockage cleared and Jerome began to shout. 'RELAX? Did he just tell me to relax?'

Tonka smiled. 'Yeah boss,' he replied quietly and backed off into the dressing room very slowly.

Soon enough Jerome realised he was standing on his own in the tunnel. A few seconds passed by. Jerome took a deep breath. He dug his hands into his tracksuit bottoms and kicked an empty 7-Up can down the tunnel. Then he went back inside the dressing room and pulled the door shut behind him. It was time for the most important team talk of his managerial career.

At ten to three the Stretford Enders ran out on to the lush green grass of Tolka Park to the encouraging cheers of their supporters in the main stand. It was a scorching hot summer's day, traditional Cup Final weather.

Luke stood on the pitch, ten yards in front of the home

dugout. He used his left hand as a sun visor and searched through the faces in the crowd. He spotted Ronald and Mrs Hendy sitting at the back of the main stand, but there was still no sign of Martina.

'Luke,' Jerome said. He and the other players had gathered at the edge of the penalty area for the customary team huddle. Luke, as captain, was crucial to the ceremony. As he jogged down the side of the pitch to join his team-mates, he also searched through the crowd for a sign of Ella. He assumed she'd come to watch the match with her mother, Mo.

'OK, Enders, listen up,' Jerome said as Luke joined his team-mates. But Jerome wasn't more than two sentences into his pep talk when he noticed Luke still scanning the main stand in a bid to locate his mother and his girlfriend. This lack of concentration annoyed him.

'Luke!' Jerome snapped impatiently.

Luke turned his attention back to Jerome. 'What?' he replied rudely.

Jerome sighed in despair. He started scratching his scalp rapidly, like a cocker spaniel searching out fleas. The other players looked on in silence. Jerome turned to Tonka. ' "What?" he says.'

Jerome marched across to Luke and eyeballed him angrily. 'Most important game of your season, career, life. That's what,' he said in a firm, but calm voice.

A stand-off ensued. Jerome maintained his icy stare. Luke felt confused. He shrugged his shoulders.

'Well?' Jerome asked.

'Well what?' Luke replied quietly.

'Are you ready to concentrate on the game?'

Luke couldn't help himself. As if by reflex his head had arched back towards the main stand even as Jerome asked the question. He quickly refocused on his manager. 'Yeah, of course. The match, the match,' he said.

It was at this point that Luke realised he was unnerving his team-mates with his erratic behaviour. The faces in the circle were a mixture of nerves, confusion and anger, apart from Daniel Popsecu's, assistant manager of the Stretford Enders and big brother to midfield maestro Ille. Daniel was still translating into Romanian for Ille. There was no way Luke could let them pin two cup final defeats on his shoulders. It was time for action.

'Come on Enders, from the start,' Luke said forcefully, clapping his hands together.

He signalled for his team-mates to form the huddle. They linked the scrum-like circle and listened carefully as Jerome ran through his standard pep talk.

Luke's heart felt like a tonne weight. Not only had his mother abandoned him on the biggest day of his football career, but his girlfriend, Ella Barnes, who also happened to be Jerome's only daughter, was nowhere to be seen either. She and her big brother Isaac's band, the Funky Starfish, were performing at the Temple Bar Music Centre that evening in the Today FM Battle of the Bands semi-final, but there was plenty of time to get from Tolka Park to Temple Bar.

Luke could hardly see straight as the huddle broke with a monstrous roar. As team captain, he walked towards the centre-circle to meet the referee and the opposing captain. He tried hard not to, but his eyes kept veering towards the main stand. Still no sign of Ella or Martina.

Suddenly Tonka jogged across his path. 'Snap out of it,' he said as he passed.

Luke turned his head to watch Tonka jog away towards the touchline. David Swayne was running in the opposite direction. 'Cup Final to play,' he said as he zoomed by.

Luke stopped dead. He nodded his head. 'Match first, shouting match later.' He walked onto the centre-circle and shook hands with the referee, linesmen and captain of Stella Maris, despite his annoyance with Ella and Martina. There was still a football match to play and win.

THE STRETFORD ENDERS
VS
STELLA MARIS

It was, in footballing terms, David versus Goliath. The Stretford Enders, runaway champions of South Dublin League Division E, but rank outsiders in the U-15 showpiece final. And Stella Maris, champions of Dublin Schoolboy League Division A, reigning All-Ireland Cup holders with a team that boasted seven Irish U-15 internationals.

'From the start, Enders,' Luke said.

Stella Maris kicked off. Immediately Luke and Ille chased after the ball like preying cheetahs. It was a blistering hot June Sunday, but both sets of players raced around the pitch at a furious pace. The first five minutes of the match passed by in a flash until Stella Maris forced a corner and flooded the penalty area with players.

'Muffin, mark up,' Alan Giles shouted.

The Maris No.7 swung a beautiful corner to the back post. It landed on the head of the lanky No.5 who had climbed above David Swayne. He powered his header low to the left. Alan Giles responded with a fine fingertip save, turning the ball round the post for another corner.

The Stella Maris supporters sensed the inevitable and began to cheer fiercely. It was time to dig in for the Enders defence. Luke somehow managed to keep tight to the No.4, who buzzed about the penalty area like a hyperactive blue-bottle. The No.7 swung in another inch-perfect cross to the back post, Alan Giles came out to punch, but the No.5's massive frame elevated him above Alan's right glove. He headed the ball into the empty net.

The Stella Maris players ran off to congratulate the No.5 who jogged across to salute their screaming fans at the bottom of the main stand. It left the penalty area full to the brim with disillusioned faces in blue jerseys. Luke found himself glancing into the crowd, hands on hips. Alan Giles sat despondent on the ground. Even Tonka was subdued.

Everyone but David Swayne. 'What are you all waiting for?' he said as he lifted Alan Giles on to his feet. Everyone watched him in silence. 'COME ON!!! I haven't come this far to give up now,' David said forcefully.

It was like an electric shock treatment administered to a dying body in a casualty room. Suddenly, energy, belief and spirit flowed throughout the veins of every Stretford Ender. The game restarted.

Predictably, Stella Maris bombed forward on the crest of a wave and tried to bury the game before half-time. This was to be expected. Thankfully the Enders had been in the same situation countless times before, all through the League Cup campaign the previous season and all through the fourteen All-Ireland Cup Ties that season. It was time for the defence to stand strong.

Edgar O'Lone and Copper Martin tackled like tigers. The Burke brothers, Muffin and Éclair, kept tight to their men on the wings and Tonka, Lofty and Leslie Ward helped out in midfield. But the player holding the whole ship together was David Swayne. He had already picked up the club award for Player of the Year and seemed to get better with each game.

'Copper, put it out,' David screamed. He had just made

another of his perfectly timed sliding tackles to save a team-mate's blushes and prevent a certain goal. Copper took no exception to David's harsh tone. He simply nodded his head in agreement and jogged back to defend the corner.

Jerome and Daniel Popsecu stood on the touchline, nervously awaiting the outcome of another corner. Reaching half-time only one goal down was crucial. 'Come on, men, stand tall,' Jerome said loudly.

This passionate remark drew a chorus of sniggers from the Stella Maris bench. Jerome turned towards them, observing the smug expressions on substitutes and manager alike. He turned back to Daniel and patted his left shoulder. 'Yeah, we'll see,' Jerome said.

Luke came back to help defend the corner. Ille was the only Enders player not inside his own penalty area. Luke watched the No.4 performing his usual angry fly routine. He decided to let him buzz unchallenged.

'Luke, mark up,' Tonka said.

It was too late. The No.7 had swung yet another pinpoint cross to the back post. The No.5 muscled Copper Martin out of his path and prepared to power a header towards goal. But this time, all he connected with was fresh air.

Luke had stolen in on the No.5's blind side and nodded the ball out to the edge of the penalty area. Now it was time for Lady Luck to intervene. Ille watched Luke's looping header glide through the air towards his chest. The No.3 moved in to challenge for the ball. Big mistake. Ille spun round at that precise moment. The No.3 took his eye off the ball for a split second and watched in horror as Ille powered away from goal with the ball at his feet.

'Out,' David Swayne said loudly.

Tolka Park watched in excitement as the skilful little Romanian skipped past the desperate lunges of the No.6 and

No.2 and raced into the Stella Maris half of the field. Luke, Lofty and Leslie plus the entire Maris team sprinted back down the pitch to catch up with Ille, who was fifty yards from goal and drifting left.

Luke pumped his arms and legs in a desperate attempt to support the counter-attack. Ille was approaching the left-hand side of the penalty area. The No.3 and No.11 were catching up fast. As they prepared to tackle Ille, Luke raised his arm. 'Ille,' he cried desperately.

Ille delivered a sublime curling cross into the penalty area. It travelled a foot off the ground and came towards Luke. He kept his eye trained on the ball and prepared to slot it past the helpless keeper. But before Luke could connect with the ball, his face drained with shock and horror.

A large, clumsy black Adidas boot stole in front of him. It all happened in slow motion. Luke watched as the ball flicked off the offending foot and hurtled into the top left-hand corner of the net, beating the keeper on his near post.

'Leslie,' Luke said quietly.

A small section of the crowd in the main stand erupted in celebration. Leslie followed the ball into the back of the net and screamed 'YESSS!!!' at the top of his lungs. He then turned and ran across to Ille and lifted him into the air. Luke sat on the ground, smiling.

'What a jammy bastard,' Lofty said. He held out his right hand to help Luke off his backside. Luke accepted the offer and commented as they walked towards the halfway line.

'One goal all season and he scores it in the All-Ireland Cup Final.'

Jerome, Daniel and the three Ender substitutes celebrated wildly on the touchline. Jerome noticed the swift transition on the Stella Maris bench. The expressions had changed from smug to glum in the space of thirty seconds. He knew on the balance of play the Enders were fortunate to be level. But he just couldn't help himself.

'Well done, men, keep standing tall,' he yelled deliberately.

Stella Maris had barely had time to restart the game when the referee blew his whistle for half-time. The sun was beginning to dip slightly in the afternoon sky as the players walked off the pitch. Luke was deep in discussion with Tonka about strategy for the second half. He didn't shoot even half a glance at the main stand before they passed off into the tunnel.

The second half was a bloody battle. Stella Maris threw everything at the Stretford Enders. Corners, free-kicks, shots from outside and inside the penalty area; they had all the possession and all the play. In fairness, on a different day they would have won by ten clear goals.

But two key factors kept the score tied at one apiece. Resolute defending and David Swayne. And there was little doubt which factor was tipping the balance. Luke had done his part. Every time the ball came up to him, he retained possession and gave the defence vital breathers. Ille looked dangerous when he got the chance to run at the Stella Maris defence and Tonka provided his predictable powerhouse display in centre-midfield.

David Swayne, however, played a superhuman game. He won everything in the air, everything on the ground. Each time a Stella Maris forward created a chance to shoot, David blocked him down. Any conceivable opening on goal, any offensive threat Stella Maris created was stamped out by the boot, body or head of David Swayne. Then with seven minutes remaining, he crowned his display. A quicksilver counter-attack by Lofty and Luke up the left wing had resulted in the Enders winning their first corner of the second half.

Leslie Ward prepared to swing it in. David Swayne decided to throw caution to the wind. He trotted up field to offer aerial presence in the opposing penalty area. Everyone inside Tolka Park could sense this was a key moment in the match. If Stella Maris could clear their lines and attack with David out of position . . .

Leslie whipped a dangerous inswinging cross to the near post. Luke and Tonka watched from the centre of the penalty area as David lost his marker, made a late diagonal run to the near post and rose majestically above the No.5 to glance his header to the far corner of the goal. Although the No.3 was protecting that part of the line, the ball was nestling in the top corner before he could even jump to head it clear.

'Ahhhhhrgghh,' Jerome said, screaming like an eight-year-old choirboy. He ran onto the pitch in celebration, kicking over the water bucket and soaking his tracksuit ends in the process. He and Daniel then danced about the touchline in delight. The Stretford Enders section of the crowd was in delirious uproar. Everyone else in the main stand sat in complete silence, unable to comprehend the possibility of defeat.

'It's not over yet,' David said calmly as his team-mates tried to embrace him. 'Concentration, Enders. Concentration.'

David jogged back down the pitch, urging his team-mates back to their positions with a glorious swoop of his arms. Luke stared at him with a funny sense of awe. Tonka was jogging alongside him, watching David with the same sense of awe and wonder. 'He's like that Braveheart geezer,' Luke said.

'I was thinking Kevin Ratcliffe myself,' Tonka replied.

Stella Maris kicked off wearily. Most of their players wandered about the pitch like mortally wounded animals. Paralysed with fear, shock and exhaustion. David broke down a desperate solo run by the No.10 inside the penalty area with an inch-perfect sliding tackle. The Stella Maris crowd and bench simultaneously screamed for a spot kick as the No.10 sprawled on to the ground like a top-drawer Hollywood stuntman. The referee waved play on. David Swayne was already moving down the pitch with the ball at his feet. Before an opposing player could make a tackle, he saw an opportunity.

David hit a superb sixty-yard cross-field pass out on to the left wing. It was a wonderfully weighted ball, landing precisely on Ille's left foot. Suddenly the Stella Maris defence, which had steamed forward in search of an equaliser, was woefully exposed. Luke didn't even have to ask for the ball. Ille slipped a wonderful through-ball between the two flat-footed centre-halves.

'Ref,' the No.5 screamed, his arm dangling in the air.

Jerome and Daniel watched in breathless anticipation as Luke steamed in on goal. In the main stand Ronald jumped to his feet in excitement. 'Come on, Luke,' he said quietly.

It was a bread-and-butter chance for Luke Farrell. He waited patiently for the advancing keeper to commit himself before coolly slotting the ball between his open legs into the empty net. It was 3–1 to the Stretford Enders and goal number forty-nine of the season for Luke. His No.7 jersey came off and was waved about in celebration.

'Mr Barnes, Mr Barnes. We've won. WE'VE WON!!!' Daniel said happily to Jerome. Jerome slumped to his knees on the lush green grass of the touchline. He seemed to be smiling, but tears were streaming down his cheeks.

Stella Maris restarted the game. But it wasn't long before the referee perched the whistle in his mouth and blew. The All-Ireland Cup Final was over.

Luke stood in the centre-circle. He watched his team-mates celebrate from afar while carrying out his captain's duty of diplomacy, shaking hands with the Stella Maris players and the referee. Everyone had gathered round David Swayne in the penalty area. He was on his knees, overcome by the moment. Alan Giles and Copper Martin helped him to his feet before Tonka launched him up on to his shoulders and led the other players as they paraded their hero to the supporters.

'Oi,' a familiar voice said. Luke felt Jerome's hand on his shoulder. They both watched the Enders crowd from the main stand invade the pitch and gather round to salute their conquering hero.

'It's his cup, you know,' Luke said.

Jerome slung his arm around Luke's shoulder. He considered his point carefully.

'Yeah, you're right. But he's not that type of kid,' he replied softly. Jerome growled playfully. He lifted Luke into an affectionate bear hug before plopping him back on to the grass and kissing his crown. He jogged back over to the touchline, leaving Luke to sit alone in the centre-circle for a while longer. He decided to savour the moment and watch the Enders crowd give David Swayne three deserved victory bumps.

After a while Luke's attention drifted back to the touch-line. He noticed Jerome standing at the dugout with a tall, thin man wearing a navy blue, Umbro promo jacket. He was completely bald on top but sported tragically uncool strands of long brown hair around the back and sides of his head. Luke had never seen the man before. But he and Jerome seemed to be sharing a joke.

Again his attention shifted. Now he was staring into the main stand. He noticed Ronald and Mrs Hendy sitting alone. He waved up to them, they waved back. No sign of Martina, no sign of Ella. Luke felt a foul gulp of anger pass up through his lungs and out his nostrils. But the stench quickly evaporated. It was time to lift the All-Ireland Cup and then it was time to celebrate.

END OF SEASON PARTY

Luke sat alone at a shiny steel table in the Bowler's Hat Café. For the second year in a row Jerome had brought the lads to the Stillorgan Bowl for their end of season party. The prizes had already been handed out.

David Swayne   – Player of the Year
Edgar O'Lone   – Most Improved Player
Muffin Burke   – Clubman of the Year
Luke Farrell   – Top Scorer (49 Goals)

The other boys were now busy bowling while Luke sat in the café dunking chunky chips in the ketchup bowl. Despite the glorious triumph at Tolka Park three hours earlier, he didn't feel like celebrating. Neither Martina nor Ella had bothered to show up. The greatest day in his footballing life and the two most important people had gone AWOL. Even Ronald had deserted him. He had left the Stillorgan Bowl half an hour earlier to drive Mrs Hendy home. Luke had felt like going with them.

'What's up with you?' Tonka said.

He and David had walked into the Bowler's Hat Café and sat down beside Luke without him noticing. He was still slumped sadly in his seat. Tonka took a handful of chips without asking while David repeated the question.

'What's the matter?'

Luke sighed wearily. 'This isn't much of a celebration.'

Tonka coated two chips with a thick sludge of ketchup. 'What did you have in mind?' he asked.

Luke straightened up in his chair. He looked up at Tonka and David, realising he had their full attention, and considered suggesting his idea. Tonka wasn't likely to object but David might prove a problem. Luke slumped back down again. 'Na, forget it,' he said.

'What? What is it?' David replied quickly.

Luke surveyed the two faces again. They both seemed determined to hear the plan. After all, anything Luke Farrell told you reluctantly had to be worth hearing.

'I'm not sure about this,' David said anxiously.

'Why?' Tonka asked.

'Well, what will Mr Barnes say?'

It was too late to discuss the issue at length. The 46A was stopped at a red traffic light, waiting to make its way off the dual carriageway. Its next stop was outside the Stillorgan Bowl. Luke tried to ease David's concerns.

'Look, we stayed for two hours. All that's left is the Quasar.'

David opened his mouth to reply. He happened to love Quasar and was a Stillorgan Bowl Hall of Fame crackshot. However, such a hideously uncool statement in front of Luke and Tonka was a risky move. David was a year younger than them and the last image he wanted to portray was that of Quasar-playing kiddie. 'Yeah, let's go. I hate Quasar anyway,' David said unconvincingly.

Tonka gave Luke a split-second glance. They both concealed tiny smiles. Half a minute later the 46A pulled up to the stop. Although David needed a helpful tug from Luke in front and a hefty nudge from Tonka behind, the boys were soon safely on board.

It was ten past eight but a copper-shaded sun was still holding court in a brazen evening sky. The 46A drove past the Stillorgan shopping centre. Luke, Tonka and David climbed the twisting staircase to a deserted top deck and claimed the back seat for themselves.

'David.' The sound of Luke's voice quickly diverted David's attention away from his view of Foley's Hardware Store. 'When we reach the door of the music centre, keep your mouth shut,' Luke said carefully.

David's face turned white as milk. He didn't know whether to feel insulted or ashamed. Luke arched his neck forward to examine the sight of Oaklands Secondary School as the 46A zoomed by. He had thirty minutes before they reached Fleet Street. Thirty minutes to prepare himself for the first fight of the evening.

The city centre was bursting with activity when the boys departed the 46A on Fleet Street. Hoards of people swarmed about the streets. The fabulous sunshine was a strong incentive to go outside but Dublin city centre was always packed nowadays, rain or shine. Especially Temple Bar.

'What time are they on?' Tonka asked.

'Nine,' Luke replied.

He and Tonka walked through Temple Bar Square side by side. David trailed a few feet behind them. The closer they came to the Temple Bar Music Centre the more negative David seemed about his chances of getting in.

'Maybe I should go home,' he said anxiously.

Luke came to an abrupt halt just as they reached the edge of Curved Street. He turned to reassure David. 'Look, relax. Ella left three names on the guest list. We'll have no problem getting in.' Luke looked into his eyes carefully. 'Are you cool?' he asked.

David nodded his head unconvincingly. Luke led them on to Curved Street. They reached the entrance of the Temple Bar Music Centre where two burly men in black bomber jackets blocked their passage inside. Neither of the men bothered to raise a smile to Luke and the lads, and both seemed more concerned with picking up a clear signal from the earpiece of their expensive headsets.

Luke wore a confident smile.

'Can I help you boys?' the older bouncer said sarcastically. Luke took this put-down in his stride.

'We're here to see the Funky Starfish. I'm on the guest list, Luke Farrell plus two.'

The bouncer wasn't impressed. He took a long scornful look at the boys. For a while, Luke didn't think he would bother to check the guest list. But eventually, he did. While the bouncer scanned the names, Luke turned to Tonka and David and nodded his head confidently.

'No Luke Farrell,' the bouncer said.

'What?' Luke replied with a genuine shriek of surprise.

He stood on tip-toes to spy the guest list. The bouncer turned the pages of the navy leather ledger into his chest to prevent him from doing so. They stared at one another for a few seconds. Luke decided to change tactics and adopted his most pitiful expression. The one he would use on Martina as a child to swindle a packet of FA Premier League stickers or a bag of Monster Munch on a visit to the shops.

'Can I see it, please?' Luke said in a semi-whimper.

The bouncer was reluctant to show him. But Luke continued with his shameless 'on the verge of tears' face. Eventually the bouncer caved in. But more out of disgust than pity. He turned the ledger around for Luke to search out his name. Luke ran the tip of his right index finger down the list of names. No joy.

'What?' he said in dismay. This was the final insult. Ella had failed to put his name on the guest list. The other Funky Starfish had filled up their spaces. But Ella had bumped Luke for somebody called Wesley Adams. 'Wesley Adams?' he said softly.

Luke stared at the list of names, wondering what to do next. Suddenly the ledger was whipped from under his nose. Older and Younger Bouncer advanced forward from the entrance with a clear purpose. Luke, Tonka and David happily retreated from their path into Curved Street. 'What happens now?' Luke said with a shocking air of innocence.

Older Bouncer couldn't help but laugh out loud. He seemed to be deriving real pleasure from Luke's misfortune. After exhausting the hilarity of the joke to a questionable extreme, he leaned forward and delivered his damning reply. 'You go home, son.'

Younger Bouncer sniggered gleefully. Tonka and David stepped back a further five feet, removing themselves from connection with Luke and his public ridicule. Luke didn't care, he had a back-up plan. 'What if we pay in?' he said enthusiastically.

The bouncers shared a quick glance. Again Older Bouncer took the lead.

'How old are you?' he said, studying Luke, Tonka and David with considerable mistrust.

The three Enders shared a split-second glance before facing Older Bouncer.

'Eighteen,' they replied in near unison.

This sounded like an under-strength Barbershop quartet; Tonka had the voice of a gruff Alaskan frontiersman, Luke that of a cocky Northside teenager waiting for puberty to kick in and David that of a weedy pre-teen choirboy.

The lads watched Older Bouncer with baited breath as he

rubbed his stubbly chin stoically. At least he was thinking it through. 'Not tonight lads,' he said finally. This was a conclusive reply. There would be no opportunity to re-negotiate.

Luke, Tonka and David drifted into the centre of Curved Street, standing about in that aimless way teenage boys do when they've been refused entry to a nightclub. They were just about to head back to Fleet Street to catch the 46A to Dun Laoghaire when a white RTE transit van pulled up on the far side of Curved Street. Luke recognised the face instantly. 'Nice one,' he said.

Tonka and David remained rooted to the same spot in Curved Street watching Luke run across to the van. He waited for the passenger door to open before introducing himself to a perplexed middle-aged man with greying hair, wearing a neat black polo-neck jumper beneath a sharp turquoise suit.

'Who's that?' Tonka said quietly. David shrugged his shoulders. Luke was locked in conversation with the man while three other men casually dressed in T-shirts and jeans, unloaded equipment from the back of the van. Cameras, a big furry microphone, headphones. The lads turned their attention back on Luke and the well-dressed man. His expression had turned from sheer shock and fear to a pleasant smile. Luke seemed to be saying goodbye to the man. He turned to the lads wearing a smile, his right thumb lifted in the air.

Tonka and David watched Luke stride back down Curved Street to the entrance of the Music Centre. He approached the bouncers confidently, who were unaware of developments with RTE.

'For the last time boys, not tonight,' Older Bouncer said firmly.

Luke wore a smug grin. 'We'll see,' he said quietly.

Luke wiggled his finger to beckon Tonka and David to his side. It was like an old cowboy movie. Luke and his posse facing off against the sheriff and his young deputy. Stalemate, the kind usually decided by hot lead or a fist fight. But Luke was playing poker, and he had four aces up his sleeve.

The two bouncers stood outside the Temple Bar Music Centre in the chilly night air. They made sure to glance into the bar every ten seconds to check on the behaviour of Luke, Tonka and David. The heavyweight support of TV personality Paul Porter and his crew, in attendance to film a slot for Starsearch 2000 – *Where are they now?* – tipped the balance in favour of Luke and the boys. Luke had gone over to the RTE van and had a quiet word with Porter, introducing himself as Ella's boyfriend and the very person who sent off Ella and Funky Starfish's audition tape to Starsearch. The Starsearch presenter did the rest. And the bouncers reluctantly stood aside. But they issued a verbal warning. One false move, and the lads would be out on their ears in a flash.

'What time is it?' Luke said.

'Five to,' Tonka replied.

'I suppose we'd better head in.' Luke picked up his glass of Coke and walked through the door that separated the bar and the venue. Ella and the Funky Starfish were about to take the stage in the semi-final of the Today FM Battle of the Bands. The venue wasn't jam-packed but there was a healthy crowd. Tonka and David wandered towards the front of the stage. It was only as the house lights dimmed that they noticed Luke had disappeared.

'Where's he gone?' David said.

Tonka searched through the faces in the crowd behind them. He located Luke at the far end of the venue, standing against a wall. He was about to suggest to David they move to join Luke when a red velvet curtain started to rise on stage. The smoke machine coughed a blanket of dry ice into the air. Tonka sipped his pint of Heineken. 'We'll stall it for one song,' he said to David.

The Funky Starfish appeared on stage one by one and kicked off their set with 'Tears Of A Clown'. Ella was last to emerge from backstage, wearing a metallic mini-skirt Martina had bought her for Christmas, knee-high black leather boots and a white belly top with a rainbow across the chest.

Luke felt a quick shudder of excitement and pride run up his spine. Every time Ella dressed for the occasion she blew him, and everybody else, away. Such a stunning outfit could usually snap Luke out of any childish sulk in seconds. And for a brief moment, he considered tossing away his bone of contention. 'Snap out of it,' he said to himself. But this was different. She had let him down badly this time. Luke was determined to remain angry. Ella had dug her own hole by missing the Cup Final. He had every right to kick up a fuss.

'Tears Of A Clown' came to an end and the audience burst into rapturous applause. Tonka and David took advantage of the lengthy interval between songs to join Luke at the back of the venue. Tonka supped his beer with a smile. He leaned into Luke's left ear and noted, 'I have to say it. She's a cracker.'

Luke shrugged his shoulders. Tonka and David turned to face the stage again as the Funky Starfish began to play 'Midnight At The Oasis'.

Luke was still clinging on to his anger like a child with a safety blanket. But he knew that Tonka was right. Ella had really come out of her shell. There was no way to put her back inside, and every other man in the world could see now the splendid beauty that had been hidden for so long beneath dungarees and Doc Martins. The mysterious name of Wesley Adams was imprinted on Luke's mind. He would never admit it to Ella, but the name Wesley Adams scared him deeply. He turned his attention on to the stage and felt a cold fear. Ella was fifty yards away and completely out of reach. He hoped this was a temporary situation.

The artists' dressing rooms in the Temple Bar Music Centre were buried deep in the basement. Luke, Tonka and David tagged along with Paul Porter and the Starsearch crew after the Funky Starfish finished their set.

'Hey, Luke,' Isaac Barnes said brightly as he walked into the dressing room. 'Congratulations man. Pop told us the score.'

Isaac shook hands with Tonka and David while Luke glanced across at Ella. Paul Porter and his crew prepared to conduct an interview. Standing beside Ella was a tall, handsome young man with thick but neatly cropped brown hair and the chiselled good looks of a Hollywood superhunk. He was wearing a dark brown suede jacket, sleek black polo-neck jumper, black corduroy flares and smart camel boots. He whispered something in her ear. She began to laugh, gazing up into his rich green eyes. He was smiling, an activity that infuriated Luke. Mystery man revealed a set of perfect pearly whites and cheekbones you could safely hang three tonne anchors from. Luke switched his attention back to Ella. She wasn't too far away from drooling on to Mystery man's boots.

'Luke,' Isaac said, waving his hands in front of Luke's face. Luke snapped out of it. He smiled at Isaac who dabbed beads of sweat from his neck with a blue hand towel. 'Great set,' Luke said. 'But what happened to "River Deep"?' he added, trying to keep up a charade of interest with a challenging question.

Isaac sat down on a large black Marshall amplifier and crossed his legs in a considered fashion. 'Yeah, top tune. But not the same without an orchestra.'

Luke's attempt to play it cool was wavering. Mystery man stood beside Ella in the intimate stance reserved for boyfriend, bodyguard, or . . .

'Oh, by the way. Have you met our new manager?' Isaac said.

Luke spun round to face him. 'Manager?' he said.

Isaac nodded his head. 'Yeah. The bloke next to Ella . . . Wesley Adams.'

The blood vessel on Luke's forehead almost exploded with rage. Tonka and David were oblivious. They joined the other Starfish for a complimentary can of Budweiser. But Luke was going nowhere. He stood on the same spot observing the interview carefully. Whenever he could, he made strong eye contact with Ella. She smiled at him, unaware of his raging anger and suspicion. Paul Porter wrapped up the interview and turned his crew round to catch a brief word with the Funky Starfish. Ella and Wesley were talking; Luke wanted to be sick. He also wanted to charge across and whack Wesley Adams one on the nose. Somehow he managed to control his temper. He waited patiently for Ella to come to him. She did so four minutes later. The prolonged delay did little to lift Luke's spirit.

'I'm really sorry,' Ella said. She wrapped her arms round Luke in a loving embrace. His own arms remained folded across his chest, his eyes as cold as ice. Ella felt the bump of his buffer against her navel. She knew something was up. 'What's the matter?' she said quietly, moving a step back from Luke.

'Can we talk outside?' he replied calmly.

Ella nodded her head in agreement. She took Luke by

the hand and guided him through the crowd of Starfish, managers, TV crew members and general hangers-on.

Tonka and David stood by the doorway. They watched Luke and Ella leave together.

'Temperamental git, Luke,' Tonka said thoughtfully. David was confused by the remark but nodded his head in agreement. He took another sip of Budweiser and tried not to wince at the awful taste.

Outside the dressing room, Ella and Luke headed along a narrow corridor towards the staircase. Wesley Adams was at the foot of the steps, talking on his mobile phone. He flashed that winning smile Ella's way. As he and Ella passed by, Luke gave Wesley a sinister stare with the banner headline message, 'I don't like you'.

Curved Street was illuminated by an assortment of blue neon lights hanging from the windows of Art-House, the building opposite the Music Centre. Luke and Ella stood outside the entrance, staring at one another in silence. Ella started to feel uncomfortable but Luke had no intention of talking.

'Luke, what's the matter?' Ella said.

No reply. Just a long icy stare.

'Have I done something wrong?' she asked.

Luke exploded on the inside. He had to turn away from her. The bouncers watched in amazement as he walked around the pavement in a funny little circle. When he had completed a revolution he held three fingers in front of Ella's face.

'One, the Cup Final, two, the guest list, and three, who's that bloke with the suede jacket?' Luke said forcefully.

Ella stood there shivering in her T-shirt and mini-skirt. She had every intention of standing up for herself, but Luke's rant was justified. His complaints about the Cup Final and the guest list were legitimate. But Wesley was an unexpected shot in the dark. Luke awaited her reply. He paced from side to side in an attempt to vent his fury and to keep warm.

Ella decided to offer an olive branch. 'Look, I'm really sorry about the match. But we had to sound-check at half five. Half an hour to get from Tolka Park to Temple Bar was too risky.'

Luke had to accept this excuse. But the guest list was unforgivable.

'. . . and the reason your name wasn't on the guest list was . . .' Ella hesitated, to Luke's utter dismay. Suddenly he could feel his heart burst into flames. She was in love with Wesley Adams. The guilt was written all over her face. '. . . we got a call from Wesley about managing the band. He offered to pay for studio time. But he wanted to see us live first.'

Luke wasn't buying this one. Wesley could have attended the first heat of the Battle of the Bands. Wesley could have watched a videotape of the Starsearch 2000 final. She was already lying to cover her cheating tracks.

'So it's all right for me to stand outside in the freezing cold when Wesley wants to see you live,' Luke said. A wonderful point came to mind. He almost screamed with excitement to make it. 'Tell me this: if Wesley is so desperate to manage you, why wouldn't he pay to see you?'

Luke made certain to raise his voice to a howling crescendo by the end of the second sentence. Ella took his damning broadside without sustaining serious damage. She simply threw her eyes to the heavens and sighed in a loud, feminine way. Luke hated this sigh. It was the same sigh Martina (and the whole of womankind, in Luke's opinion) employed as a sneaky time-out in an argument – that they were losing – with their partner. Luke continued pacing the pavement from side to side. Ella stood perfectly still, carefully tracking his erratic movement.

Luke could see it in her eyes. Now it was time for the 'I won't talk to you until you calm down and behave like an adult' silence. Another classic Martina Farrell tactic. She and Ella knew the longer this silence ensued, the more likely Luke was to explode in fury, tipping the balance in their favour.

'Stop playing your little game, Ella,' he said impatiently.

Ella glanced away from him casually. 'You're the one acting like a child,' she replied softly.

Luke gasped dramatically. He pointed at his chest. 'I'm the child?'

'Yes.'

'Me?'

Stalemate. Luke set off on another circular voyage of Curved Street. As he moved away from her, Ella muttered something. It was deliberately loud enough for him to hear.

'Me, me, me.'

Luke looked back at her sharply. 'Excuse me?' he said.

'Shut up, Luke. I'm sick of listening to you moan,' Ella replied with an exhausted groan. 'You're like a spoilt kid,' she added.

Luke watched her disappear back inside the Music Centre. He stood alone in Curved Street, face to face with the two bouncers who sported smug grins. Luke quickly followed after Ella, but she was marching away at a tremendous pace. He finally caught up with her at the top of the basement staircase.

'Why am I spoilt? I'm not the one who forgets about Cup Finals and guest lists,' he protested strongly.

Ella groaned with despair. 'Luke, the world doesn't revolve around you and your football career.'

They stared at one another. Luke wasn't sure how he felt

any more but Ella was in complete control of her emotions. She reached out her hand and caressed his cheek lovingly. 'I'm sorry, OK? I'm sorry about the match and I'm sorry about the guest list,' Ella said.

Luke smiled. At last the poor girl had seen sense.

'But I have my own career to think of,' she concluded bluntly.

That was that. Luke jerked his face away from the palm of her hand. He adopted his sulky expression and stormed down the staircase.

Back in the dressing room, Tonka and David were deep in discussion with Cedric and Isaac about the plentiful supply of complimentary Budweiser. Luke made an open announcement. 'I'm going home. Are you coming?'

Tonka and David felt the party atmosphere deflate instantly. Luke's expression was sullen. Isaac was determined to change it. He slung his arm around Luke's shoulder. 'Luke. Cup's in the bag, exams in the bag, Battle of the Bands in the bag. Let your hair down, our kid.' Isaac handed him a can of Budweiser. Seconds later Ella appeared outside the ajar door of the dressing room. Wesley Adams quickly ditched a conversation with Paul Porter to join her.

Luke stared deeply into her eyes. It was time for him to leave. 'Another time, Isaac,' he replied.

Luke turned to Tonka and David who looked to be enjoying themselves no end. They had just won the All-Ireland Cup Final. Last Friday, Luke and Tonka had their final Junior Cert exam. It was the summer, time to cut loose, have it large. Luke didn't fancy sitting beside two glum faces on the 46A. Especially if he was the one who had caused them to look so unhappy.

'You two stay. I'll see you tomorrow.'

Luke handed the can of Budweiser to Tonka with a knowing

nod. He didn't wait for a reply and walked straight out of the dressing room. Ella didn't try to stop him as he passed by her and Wesley Adams. That suited Luke fine.

From Bad to Worse

Luke sat on the engine seat of the 46A, his feet sprawled across the double seat opposite. He was trying to remember the last time he had sat alone on a bus feeling sorry for himself. It was probably during the Easter holidays after a Junior Cert revision bust-up with Ella.

It was unusual for them to go a full week without a blazing row. But tonight's argument was different. Over the space of twelve months and countless fights, this was the first time one person had been totally in the wrong. Ella had let him down. She'd abandoned Luke on the biggest day of his life. But what made it worse was the fact that she didn't seem too bothered.

'Weasel Adams,' Luke said in a low scornful voice.

The 46A powered along Montague Avenue. Luke didn't pay attention as it zoomed by Mrs Hendy's house. He was busy allowing his imagination to run wild. It was reaching some ridiculous conclusions concerning Ella and Weasel.

The bus had been stationary for three minutes and the few remaining passengers had disembarked. Luke snapped out of his daydream and focused on the driver who stood at the top of the corridor. 'Did you miss your stop?' he asked.

'No,' Luke replied. 'Why?'

The driver reached into his cockpit and turned the ignition key. The engine stopped humming. 'Go get some sleep, kid.'

Luke stepped off the 46A with a stern expression. He felt

that the driver's last comment was an insult of some sort although he couldn't quite work out how. Eight orange streetlamps evenly spread along the crumbling pavement lit the far side of the avenue. Luke swung his head from left to right before crossing from one pavement to the other.

The sight of Ronald and Martina standing on the steps outside the front door helped to brighten his mood a little. Luke waved to them, but neither Ronald nor Martina spotted him thirty yards down the avenue. Luke stood still for a moment and watched as Martina allowed Ronald to depart without her customary goodnight peck-on-the-cheek. He jumped into his Citroën and drove off with minimal fuss. Martina didn't bother to watch him leave. Luke had a bad feeling. Something was wrong.

The formidable anger Luke had stored up inside for his confrontation with Martina subsided as he climbed the staircase to the first floor landing. The house was statuesque as he quietly shut the living room door behind him. Martina was sitting behind the Packard Bell PC at the kitchen table. Two large piles of IT textbooks were stacked to the left and right of the monitor. The blue glow of the screen rebounding off her cheeks was the only illumination in the house.

'What time do you call this?' she said firmly.

Perfect. What a way to round off a miserable evening. Martina had the audacity to interrogate him about arriving home at 11pm even though, hours earlier, she had missed the most important football match of his life.

Luke's dormant anger suddenly erupted and spewed from his mouth in a frenzied counter-attack. 'Never mind the time. What about my match?' he said angrily.

Martina was still glued to the screen. She tapped away at the keyboard and double-clicked the mouse before answering. 'Well, I'm sorry about that. But it was unavoidable.'

Luke felt like screaming. That was her explanation. 'It' was unavoidable. Would it be too much for her to elaborate on what 'it' was?

'What was unavoidable?' said Luke.

Martina didn't answer him straight away. When she finally managed to tear her attention away from the screen, she uttered one simple word. 'Work.'

Luke sighed in frustration. This was the final straw. He could no longer be bothered with Martina and Ella. Arguing with them was like translating mushy love letters from Hungarian into Chinese. 'I'm going to bed,' he said bitterly before marching off towards his bedroom door.

'Luke, wait a second,' Martina replied quickly.

'What?' he snapped.

'I need a word.'

'Finally,' Luke thought to himself. It was only right that Martina felt guilty. If any natural justice existed in the universe she would now beg his forgiveness, bribe him with cash or an expensive gift, or, better yet, relieve him from washing-up duty for the next three months.

Luke stood outside his bedroom door with his hand perched on the doorknob waiting for Martina to face him. She tapped away at the keyboard. Somehow, he couldn't imagine her falling on her knees to beg for his forgiveness. Martina double-clicked the mouse again. The PC's hard drive crackled into action. Meanwhile, she stood up from her chair and flicked on the living room light. She stretched out her back, walked to the fridge door and lifted out a carton of orange juice. Was she doing this on purpose? Surely she knew how annoying her unexplained silence was? Luke predictably lost his cool.

'What is it?' he shouted angrily.

Martina turned towards him sharply. She seemed quite upset.

'Don't shout at me,' she replied defensively.

Yet another silence ensued. Luke felt like banging his head on the bedroom door. Martina stood by the fridge, sipping her orange juice. Luke lost it altogether. He rushed across the room and slammed the fridge door shut. 'Look, you wanted a word, right?' he said.

Martina nodded her head.

'Then what is it?'

Luke stood waiting. Martina placed the orange juice carton on the table top. She seemed to take a deep breath of unfeasible proportions. This 'word' was to do with something serious. Luke began to feel nervous. He watched his mother's mouth carefully, willing the words out. Finally they came. 'Ronald and I have split up,' she said softly.

Luke couldn't believe it. His shoulders slumped sadly; it felt as though they had plunged below his kneecaps. Now it was Martina desperate for him to speak. She waited patiently, but he had nothing to say. She tried to prompt him. 'Well?' she said.

Luke couldn't bring himself to look into her eyes. He spun round unsteadily and walked to his bedroom door. He took a moment to compose himself, then pressed his hand down on the handle.

'We'll talk tomorrow,' Martina said.

Luke didn't bother to reply. He opened the door and disappeared inside his bedroom. Martina stood by the fridge for a while longer. But she didn't have the time to sit about worrying. The final exams for Second Year Information Technology were three weeks away. Martina had completed all the practical coursework and was well on her way to a pass. Over the last two years she had grown from a bashful technophobe to an ambitious, confident, career mad, go-getter. She was determined to achieve a distinction. This meant long hours. But that was life. You can only get out what you put in. And no one could accuse Martina Farrell of not putting in.

Luke lay wide awake on his bed. Sleep seemed a million miles away. His mind was buzzing like a neon sign outside a motel, still sorting out the facts of Sunday evening. Ella and Weasel Adams, Ronald and Martina. What was happening to his life?

Another thing keeping him awake was the sound of Martina punching the keys of the computer. She didn't seem all that upset with the end of an eighteen month romance. 'Why?' was the million dollar question.

Although Luke didn't get to sleep until three thirty am, he took three precautions to make sure he was up at quarter to eight the next morning. He set his alarm clock, left the bedroom window slightly ajar and the curtains drawn. It worked.

Luke took a quick shower, dressed and then hurried into the kitchen for breakfast. Martina sat on the couch, skimming through the pages of an IT textbook.

'Morning,' she said brightly.

Luke didn't reply. His plan was underway. The sleepless hours of Sunday night and Monday morning had not gone to waste. Luke had worked out a suitable mode of revenge against Martina and Ella. It was time for them to feel the force of the silent treatment. They had long since employed this ghastly weapon against him. But now it was their turn to suffer the wrath of silence.

Luke filled his cereal bowl with Frosties, milk and a neatly sliced banana. Four minutes into the silent treatment, he threw occasional glances in Martina's direction. He smiled. She had a luminous yellow marker in her hand to underline passages of text in the book. Luke sniggered quietly. It was working. All he had to do was eat his breakfast. A few more minutes passed. Luke shovelled spoonful after spoonful of Frosties into his mouth and kept a subtle eye on Martina's movements about the house. She brushed her hair, put on her leather jacket, stuffed two IT textbooks into her bag and opened the living room door.

'Bye,' she said casually, looking back at Luke.

The living room door shut tight. Luke stopped chewing. This was the first time he'd used the silent treatment. He wasn't quite sure what to do next. He listened carefully to Martina walking down the staircase. She bumped into Mrs Hendy by the front door. From the muffled snippets Luke could make out they were engaged in a cheerful conversation. The front door opened, then it closed.

Luke darted across to the bay window. Martina walked up Montague Avenue, reading a textbook. This wasn't right. He expected her to be glancing back at the house remorsefully.

'I don't believe this,' Luke said loudly. He slumped back to the kitchen table. He felt a sudden loss of appetite. It was true. Martina and Ronald were finished. Luke hadn't quite believed it. Somehow he thought it was like Ella and Weasel Adams. A facet of his over-productive imagination. But this break-up was a reality.

The silent treatment had proved a resounding failure. Perhaps it was time to hear another side of the story. Luke dumped his breakfast bowl in the kitchen sink and went into his bedroom to grab his house keys. He needed to talk to Ronald.

It was another superb summer's day outside. Bright sunshine, blue skies and a cool breeze had become par for the course during the months of May and June. Luke decided to leave the 46A behind and took the long route to Dun Laoghaire College via Harbour Road. The walk should have proved useful. It would give him the chance to sort out the mess of details swirling round his head. But by the time he reached the main college driveway, it still made no sense to him.

Luke stood to one side, allowing a black Nissan Micra to pass by. A refreshing gust of wind blew across his face. 'Why?' he murmured quietly.

While the Micra manoeuvred out of the driveway onto Baker's Corner, Luke slowly started down the long and winding Tarmac road.

Why were they splitting up? A very simple but important question. Ten days earlier, Martina and Ronald had sat in the living room discussing a summer holiday. Ronald had brought round holiday brochures and made the suggestion of Florida. Luke's interest in the discussion had peaked at the mention of such an exotic destination.

'Why?' Luke whispered to himself again.

Martina and Ronald saw one another every day of the week. Ronald took the three of them out to Marcel's Carvery in Killiney for Sunday dinner every couple of weeks. Martina still laughed at his stupid jokes, listened to his monotonous tales of computer repairs and injected a semblance of style into his wardrobe.

So why split up?

Luke found the car park of Dun Laoghaire College virtually deserted. The only car in sight was Ronald's tiny orange Citroën. He didn't know why, but this depressing picture brought a tear to his eyes. He headed towards the main building.

Luke stood at the ajar door of room twelve, staring in at Ronald. He was alone, sitting at a workstation, tinkering with the insides of a hard drive.

The gentle hum of computing was the only noise for five minutes. Luke could have watched, unnoticed, for another hour or so if Ronald hadn't suddenly spun round in his swivel chair. Before he opened his mouth to speak, he saw something in Luke's eyes. Disappointment.

Sadness and regret covered Ronald's face. An expression sorely absent in the face of Martina. Luke wandered across the room. Ronald watched him all the way.

'I missed you last night. Were you out?' Ronald said quietly.

Luke didn't answer. He just stared at Ronald sadly.

'Are you OK?' Ronald asked kindly.

Luke shook his head. 'What happened?' he said eventually.

Ronald tapped his fingers against the workstation table top in a slow, steady rhythm. Luke waited patiently for an answer. Ronald stared at him with an understanding smile. 'Let's get a bite,' he said in his thick Dutch accent.

Korky's Chip Shop was neatly hidden on a narrow road that hugged the coastline, two miles south of Dun Laoghaire harbour. Luke and Ronald would visit Korky's every Sunday lunchtime. Right after an Enders match and before returning home to Martina. Korky's was a well-guarded secret between Luke and Ronald. The chips were exquisite and the quarter-pounders with cheese beyond compare throughout the world.

'Coke,' Ronald said.

He placed a can beside Luke. They were sitting on the broad granite wall overlooking a tiny, secluded beach hidden from the main expanse of Dublin Bay. The scorching sunshine had drawn a large crowd to the idyllic stretch of sand. Children laughed, splashed and screeched on sand and water. Teenage gangs giggled and shouted, and portable radios crackled out hits from the last four decades.

Ronald ploughed into his grub with gusto. He munched through thick chips soaked in salt and vinegar and took three large chunks from his quarter-pounder. Obviously the break-up was affecting Luke and his appetite more than anyone else. He was yet to open his brown paper bag, let alone eat. He stared at Ronald. 'Aren't you upset?' he said quietly.

Ronald stopped chewing. He laid his lunch beside him on the wall and squinted at Luke. The sun was obstructing his eyesight so badly he had to look away. Ronald stared out at the calm surf in front of him. Luke noticed a sad grin attached to his lips.

'Of course I'm upset . . .' Ronald said softly. He sipped from his can of Fanta orange. '. . . but that won't help things.'

'Why?' Luke replied.

Ronald ran the tip of his right index finger back and forth across his moustache. He was thinking hard about his answer. 'Luke, sometimes . . . things change,' he said.

It was a sincere but inadequate answer. Luke knew it to be the truth. Ronald never told lies, it wasn't in his nature.

'But why now? Right out of the blue,' Luke said. 'One minute you're talking about holidays to Florida and the next you're splitting up.'

Ronald went back to munching his chips. Luke's appetite was still non-existent.

'Luke,' Ronald said between slurpy chews. 'Your mother is moving on.'

'What does that mean?' Luke replied quickly. He looked to Ronald for an answer. But he just sat there eating his chips, staring sadly into the sea. Luke didn't say 'oh', but that's how he felt. Martina moving on referred to Ronald. She no longer loved him.

Luke felt guilty. He reached across and swapped his piping-hot brown paper bag for Ronald's vinegar-soaked, chipless relic. They smiled at one another and watched in silence as the glory of a warm and sunny summer's day failed to burst through the miserable bubble encasing both of them in sadness.

It was quarter to two in the afternoon when Ronald and Luke left the beach outside Korky's Chip Shop. Luke sat in the passenger seat of the Citroën, waiting for Ronald to dump the empty brown paper bags and tin cans in a nearby litter bin.

When Ronald got inside the car, he took great care to wipe his hands clean on an old tea-towel underneath his seat. Discussions on the matter of the break-up seemed to be closed. But Luke had other ideas.

'Can I ask you a favour?' he said.

Ronald turned to him wearing a bright smile.

'Talk to me ma,' Luke said.

Ronald kept his smile, but shook his head to signal an emphatic no. He turned the key in the ignition and started the engine. Luke wasn't giving up. He grabbed the steering wheel and turned it towards him.

'Please,' Luke said desperately. 'Just give it a go.'

Ronald stared at him for a while. He shut off the Citroën's engine. This explanation was going to be incredibly hard. He trained his eyes on the narrow road ahead, desperate to avoid the matter at hand.

Ronald adored Luke. He was like a son, little brother and best friend rolled into one. But he knew the facts of the matter. He didn't want to say it, but there was no hope for him and Martina. 'Luke, I love your mother. But she doesn't love me,' Ronald said sadly.

End of discussion. He put his hand to the key in the ignition. But Luke wasn't giving up so easily. He grabbed the steering wheel again and said, 'Yeah, but how do you . . .'

'. . . because I know,' Ronald said, cutting in angrily in a loud and severe tone.

It was the first time in a year and a half Luke had heard any sign of anger or distress in Ronald's voice. He turned his head away from Luke, obviously embarrassed and ashamed by his outburst.

'I'm sorry for shouting,' Ronald said without looking Luke's way.

It was horrible. Luke felt like crying. Martina had destroyed the poor man. He was putting a brave face on it but in that short outburst Luke could sense the true depth of his despair. 'It's OK,' Luke replied softly.

Ronald finally plucked up the courage to turn and look at him. They smiled at one another. But it was a smile drenched in sadness. This was the end of a beautiful friendship.

Luke went all the way back to Dun Laoghaire College with Ronald. He insisted a visit to David Swayne, who lived nearby, was on his agenda for the afternoon. It was an obvious lie. But Luke was more concerned with fooling himself than Ronald. The real reason he'd stayed in the car all the way up Harbour Road when he could have easily jumped out at Montague Avenue was that he wanted to spend some time with Ronald. Luke could never admit that publicly, but it was the truth.

'Can I call over tomorrow?' he said as they both jumped out of the car.

Ronald's face froze. He shut the car door. Luke could feel that familiar chill; more bad news on the way. 'Well, the thing is . . .' Ronald said. He didn't want to go on.

'What?' Luke replied, prompting him to continue.

'I'm moving back to Utrecht.'

It should have stung like a shower of stings from a swarm of angry bees. But this latest bombshell seemed surprisingly mild in the context of the last two days. Luke wasted no time with his follow-up questions. 'When are you going?' he said.

The wind blew fiercely across the deserted car park. Ronald held his stare bravely. 'Today,' he said.

Luke didn't flinch. 'What time?'

'Er, I sail from Rosslare at 9pm.'

A sad silence. Ronald folded his arms across the roof of the car. Luke did likewise. 'Have you packed?' he said. Ronald shook his head. Luke glanced at the ground. He looked back up at Ronald. 'Can I help?' he said.

Ronald smiled. He nodded his head. And that was that.

They walked towards the main building together. The sun was perched high in the afternoon sky. The overpowering heat had dulled a little, thankfully, and the gusty winds played the part of natural air conditioner. The afternoon trickled by at a slow pace. Luke helped Ronald pack office supplies, a broken Epson scanner, a case of CDs and floppy disks and a cardboard box filled with textbooks and manuals into the back seat of his tiny orange Citroën.

After Dun Laoghaire College they went to the Seafront Vistas apartment complex which was nestled nicely behind Salthill & Monkstown Dart station. By 5pm, the Citroën's boot was bulging with a woefully tasteless wardrobe of clothing. Ronald was heading home to Holland for the summer. It was a welcome break, purposely designed to allow him breathing space. He had a tough decision to make, return to Dublin in September or make a clean break somewhere else? Luke realised things were bad but he still held out a smidgen of hope Ronald would return and reunite with Martina.

Ronald stuffed one last sports bag full of clothes into the boot and shut it tight. He and Luke stood in the residents' car park. It was time to say goodbye.

'You have my e-mail address?' Ronald said.

Luke waved a slip of white paper with his right hand.

Ronald nodded his head. 'You will write?' he asked.

'Yeah,' Luke replied.

It was an awkward moment. But more for Luke than Ronald. In the end, inhibition disappeared and he rushed forward with his arms spread wide. Ronald cradled him with the loving embrace of a father, big brother and best friend rolled into one. 'Whatever happens in the future, I'll always call you my friend,' he said gently. Luke looked up at him. He knew he had a tear running down his left cheek but he didn't care.

'I'll miss you,' he said.

Ronald smiled. It was time to go. Luke took three paces back on to the pavement and watched Ronald climb into the Citroën. He held a thumb aloft as the engine started. Ronald raised his right hand in a wave before slowly manoeuvring the car down the driveway. Luke found it hard to breathe as it crawled towards the main road. Then, without warning, the car came to a sudden stop. The driver's window rolled down. 'Luke,' Ronald shouted.

Luke sprinted up the street after the car. When he arrived at the ajar window Ronald held his left hand out. 'You forgot this,' he said.

Luke took a brown Levi's bag from Ronald. As soon as he

had the bag, the Citroën pulled away. He stood in the middle of the road staring at the bag, then back at the disappearing car. An echoey honk of the horn signalled Ronald's final departure. Only now did Luke think of looking inside the bag. It was an unbelievable sight. He held an orange football jersey up to the sunlight, allowing the bag to fall on to the ground. Startled streams of oxygen and carbon dioxide passed each other on the way in and out of his lungs. It was a Dutch national team jersey from the World Cup in France 1998 with the name Davids and the number 16 printed on the back.

Ronald had worn the jersey to every game of the finals and had managed to get the entire Dutch squad to autograph it before the epic semi-final against Brazil in Marseilles. This was one of his most prized possessions. It normally hung with pride of place in a glass frame above the fireplace on his living room wall. Luke understood exactly how much the jersey meant to Ronald. And yet he was prepared to give it up without any self-praising song or dance routine. Now, more than ever, Luke felt Martina was cheating him out of a truly great stepfather. He glanced at his watch.

'Not without a fight,' he said quietly. Luke picked up the brown Levi's bag and stuffed the jersey back inside. He had no time to spare. It was the Bloomfield Shopping Centre or bust.

The Bloomfield Shopping Centre was a ten minute walk from the Seafront Vistas apartment complex. Luke didn't have any time to waste on a leisurely stroll through the suburban streets of Dun Laoghaire. He jogged at a tidy pace instead and entered the shopping centre through the first floor car park. He caught his breath on the travolator as it slowly slid him towards the ground floor. He was still working out the best verbal approach for his desperate plea to Martina. However, the sentiment was set in stone . . . 'Give Ronald another chance.'

Luke glanced at his watch. Quarter past five. Apart from Martina, a couple of cleaners and half a dozen other members of staff, Boots would be deserted. A perfect, private setting for their mother-son heart-to-heart.

The shop fronts along the ground floor gradually crept into sight as the travolator descended. Luke was standing behind a chubby blonde woman. The creaky metal floor beneath him slouched slowly forward.

The shock sound of cutlery crashing against a floor turned Luke's attention to Gino's Café, off to his far left. He was almost sucked under with the metal floor beneath his feet as the travolator reached the ground. He stumbled off the creaky appliance, unable to tear his gaze from Gino's Café.

'Stupid cow,' he whispered softly.

Martina was sitting at a white marble coffee table outside Gino's. Seated opposite her was a thin but handsome man with dark brown hair and the occasional streak of grey. Beneath his neatly shaven jaw he wore a spotless and expensive-looking blue shirt and navy silk tie, a grey tailored suit and shiny black leather shoes.

Luke crept up to a nearby public phone box alongside the travolator so he could maintain his vigil undercover. The man leaned across the table and whispered into Martina's right ear. She smiled and chuckled pathetically. The man moved his head away. He wore a smug grin.

'Stupid cow,' Luke said slowly.

It felt like his best friend had poisoned Luke's pre-match bottle of Lucozade Sport and laughed as he watched Luke lower it back. The same stupid question popped inside his mind. 'Why is this happening?' Luke felt as though his whole life was turning upside down.

Martina and the mystery man shared a kiss.

'In public, without any shame or guilt,' Luke thought to himself. He felt queasy. This wasn't like his mother. For a second, he wanted to turn back and run home to Montague Avenue. It was too painful to stand by and watch. But anger soon knocked sadness from his mind. 'Alright cow. See how you like this,' Luke said under his breath.

Martina sat outside Gino's, happily sipping the drains of her cappuccino. She couldn't help but smile. It seemed like a century since she'd smiled. But her happiness soon passed.

'Luke,' Martina said.

He was twenty feet away and didn't hear her. But Luke walked up to the table with a determined expression on his face. Martina could feel the sweat forming on her brow. But this was no time to panic.

'What brings you up this way?' she asked brightly.

Luke fixed a stare. 'Just passing,' he replied casually.

Martina studied his football jersey carefully. She was sure it didn't belong to Luke but she had seen it somewhere before. Suddenly it dawned on her. Ronald's living room wall. She stared into Luke's eyes. Now they both understood the situation.

Initially Martina hoped to bribe Luke with a tenner. Take Ella to the pictures, rent a few videos, buy a copy of Loaded or FHM and go home. Jonathan had popped outside a few minutes earlier to make a business call on his mobile. With a bit of luck, he and Luke might avoid contact. But now, having seen the jersey, Martina realised Luke was staying put. She attempted to explain.

'Listen . . .' she said.

Luke didn't interrupt her. He just maintained his stare. It was Martina who bottled it. Guilt had finally breached her defences. She and Luke remained still and silent, involved in a tentative game of cat and mouse. But now a shabby dog wandered in from the street.

'Excuse me,' he said, gently moving past Luke.

Martina let out a nervous sigh as Jonathan sat back down. He was unaware of the situation and simply picked up where they'd left off; smiling at her, caressing her palms. Martina's smile was gone; she gently tugged her hands away.

'Jonathan,' Martina said. 'This is my son, Luke. Luke, this is Jonathan D'Argo.'

It was quite a shock for Jonathan. But he quickly adapted to the situation and smiled, revealing a set of pearly whites identical to those possessed by Weasel Adams.

'Pleased to meet you, Luke,' Jonathan said politely.

Martina knew what was coming. Jonathan held out his hand while Luke shot an arrow-like stare through him. There was no question of him smiling, replying politely or shaking hands. Martina was fuming. But she had no choice other than to sit there and soak it up. She was in the wrong this time and Luke saw no need to obey her normal standards of decorum and good manners.

He was after revenge and justice. And he got it.

Martina and Jonathan squirmed beneath his stonewall stare for well over a minute. Silence, an unaffected stance, even a sneer of his upper lip. He ended the torture with a scathing remark to Jonathan.

'Your food is crap.'

This was way out of line. Martina had to respond.

'Luke,' she said angrily.

'No way, Mother, not today,' Luke said to himself. He walked away from Gino's Café and left the Bloomfield

Shopping Centre through the ground floor exit. His ultra-optimistic hope of Martina and Ronald reconciling lay in ruins. The only thing left to do was throw rocks off the harbour wall. One sure-fire way to relieve the pain inside his heart.

Turnaround has to be Fair Play

By any set of standards, Monday was a rotten day. Luke stood on Dun Laoghaire harbour wall, flinging rock after rock into the swirl and whoosh of the water below. He noticed the dwindling pile of rocks at his feet and began to realise his decision to come to the harbour and throw rocks into the Bay was pretty much spur of the moment. It didn't help to ease the pain or take his mind off Jonathan D'Argo. However, there was one incident Luke remembered about his visit to the Bloomfield Shopping Centre. The scathing insult he'd fired at D'Argo. Even before Martina had introduced them outside Gino's Café, Luke had recognised his smug grin from the cereal box sitting next to the microwave at home.

D'Argo was the owner of a successful chain of organic food stores. He was a self-made millionaire and had fifteen shops across the country. Martina had started to shop in D'Argo's three months ago after reading an article on the horrors of genetically modified food in the *Sunday Independent*. Suddenly, their cupboards were filling up with bags of brown rice, lentils, organic carrots and sprouts.

Now Martina was filling up on D'Argo. This could wreak havoc on Luke's stomach. Jonathan D'Argo didn't seem the sort of man who'd happily watch the Enders play each Sunday morning and follow it up with a trip to Korky's Chip Shop. Luke dreaded to think what culinary torture a Jonathan–Martina coupling would inflict on him. It

certainly wouldn't involve fortnightly trips to Marcel's
Carvery.

Luke turned his head to the rock pile by his feet. Two rocks
remained. He picked them up together and flung them into
the water simultaneously. They impacted with a loud clunk.
The sun was beginning to dip a little in the early evening sky
and a chilly breeze was gaining momentum. Luke wandered
back along the harbour wall, carrying the brown Levi's bag
under his arm.

Montague Avenue was awash with heavy traffic travelling
north and south. Luke weaved his way through the two
parallel lines of stationary vehicles and fished his front door
key from the pocket of his tracksuit bottoms.

The sound of cheerful chat and laughter greeted him as
he shut the front door behind him. He froze on the spot and
listened carefully for a moment to distinguish the voices
coming from the back parlour. There was a deep booming
male voice sharing the space with Mrs Hendy's refined
tones. Luke edged forward quietly, straining to hear.

Suddenly, the parlour door swung open. Mrs Hendy
walked into the hall. 'Ah, Luke,' she said brightly. Luke felt
deeply embarrassed by the cat-burglar-style stance he had
adopted. He quickly straightened himself up. 'You have a
visitor,' Mrs Hendy continued.

Before Luke could ask who it was, Jerome walked into the
hall from the back parlour, sipping from a china teacup.

'What happened to you last night?' he said.

Luke was caught cold. Jerome was referring to his double
disappearance. First from the Stillorgan Bowl and then from
the Temple Bar Music Centre. Luke had a whole set of other
problems before him.

'I felt sick,' he said defensively.

Luke walked by Jerome and Mrs Hendy into the kitchen and ran the cold tap over a tall glass.

'I guarantee you'll feel better in a minute,' Mrs Hendy said brightly.

Luke sank the glass of water with one steady gulp. He turned around to face Jerome and Mrs Hendy. They were both smiling with vicarious pleasure. Luke wasn't so sure. He was becoming accustomed to bad news following him round like a phantom raincloud. Whatever Jerome or Mrs Hendy were about to say would more than likely make matters worse.

'What?' asked Luke solemnly.

Jerome gulped down the drains of tea and handed the empty china teacup to Mrs Hendy. He looked at Luke with a proud grin and pulled a chair from beneath the kitchen table.

'I think you'd better sit down,' he said.

Football matches can change in a matter of seconds. So too can lives. Luke sprinted down Montague Avenue as if pursued by a gang of marauding T-1000 terminators. He attracted the angry honk of a 75's horn as he tore across Harbour Road, despite the green traffic light.

Standing far ahead on the other side of Harbour Road was Tonka Matthews. They raced from opposite ends of the street to meet somewhere in the middle. They stared at one another, desperately trying to suck air into their lungs. Expressions of uncertainty turned to delirious joy. Luke took a running jump into Tonka's arms as if they were celebrating the winning goal in a cup final.

'Yeeessssss,' they screamed at the top of their lungs.

Passers-by watched in bewilderment. Luke and Tonka danced around the pavement, arms flailing in celebration.

They screamed 'yes' and whooped for joy. At one point they slumped on their knees and looked at one another laughing. The bout of madness ended with Tonka hoisting Luke on to his sturdy shoulders. They paraded up Harbour Road singing a song.

'Everton, Everton,
We're gonna play-a-a for EVERTON.'

CELEBRATION

When sanity finally returned to Luke and Tonka, they hopped on to a 46A and went to visit David Swayne.

Earlier that day Luke had pretended to be visiting David so he could spend more time with Ronald. But now he had a good reason to keep that promise. Well, probably the best reason in the world.

'I can't believe it,' Luke said happily.

He had muttered those same four words on several occasions over the last two days. But this was, by far, in the happiest context. He and Tonka sat on the front seats of the top deck of the 46A, both staring into space. Already the dreams of glory were taking over. The tannoy crackle of the Z-Car theme tune, the roar of the Goodison Park faithful. Luke forming a clinical partnership up front with Francis Jeffers. Tonka becoming a midfield man of steel to rival and eventually surpass Roy Keane. Dramatic FA Cup Semi-finals, triumphant European campaigns, Ireland caps, a World Cup Final or three.

It was all too much to handle.

As a result, Luke and Tonka missed their bus stop by two clear miles. This meant a long walk back along the Stillorgan dual carriageway which gave them the opportunity to clear their minds.

Jerome had visited Tonka's home first with the good news. Then on to Luke, and now he was having a word with David

Swayne. The details divulged regarding Everton's interest were scant. But suffice to say, a scout called Terry Culshaw had watched the All-Ireland Cup Final and wanted to offer Luke, Tonka and David a two-day trial at their youth academy.

'Everton . . .' Tonka said. ' . . . Everton are interested in us.'

Luke smiled. 'Yeah, why not?' he replied confidently.

They walked past a small row of shops situated on a secluded slip road and cut down a narrow laneway that led to Merrion Park Estate. A hundred yards away, Jerome was coming out of David's front garden. He said goodbye to David, who stood outside the porch door, then jumped into his Ford Probe.

'I know someone who'll be sick as a dog,' Tonka said happily with a knowing nod.

'I wouldn't count on it,' Luke replied. 'He's bound to come up with some kind of excuse.' He adopted a stuffy-nosed, southside hardman accent and said, 'As if I'd play for Everton.' This impersonation made Tonka hopping mad. He knew it was accurate and it helped stoke the flames of his ongoing fury.

Tonka whacked a massive set of knuckles into a spade-sized palm. 'Please God. Let him say that,' he said.

Luke smiled. He would be interested in seeing how that encounter would turn out. They continued on up Merrion Grove. Jerome's Ford Probe was long gone by the time they entered David's front garden.

Tonka stood out of sight in a space between the front window and the porch. Luke rang the doorbell. He waited patiently for someone to answer. A large grin appeared on his face as the porch door slid open.

'What do you want, Honchee?' Peter Swayne, David's older, bully of a brother, stood tall in the porch. He stared

down at Luke, trying to evoke some of that fearsome intimi-
dation he had once held over him. Luke actually felt sorry for
Swayne. It was like Barney the dinosaur threatening to beat
you up for your dinner money.

'Hear the good news?' Luke said with a smile.

Swayne tutted loudly. 'Big deal, who wants to play for
Everton?'

At this point, Tonka slid into view. Peter Swayne turned
white as a sheet. He lurched backwards like a startled pigeon,
smacking his shoulder blades against the front door with
fright.

'I'm sorry, what did you say?' Tonka said politely.

Swayne kept a careful eye on Tonka as he pushed the front
door open behind him. He was certain a lightning-quick
right hook or smothering choke-hold was on its way. 'David.
It's for you,' Swayne shouted. He gladly retreated inside the
front door. Luke and Tonka looked at one another, smiling.
Maybe this wasn't such a rotten day after all.

The boys could hear approaching footsteps. They watched
David trundle down the staircase. He appeared at the front
door wearing his red Liverpool jersey and walked outside the
porch with a smile a mile wide plastered across his face. He
kissed the crest on his jersey. 'COME-ON-YOU-REDS,' he
sang.

Tonka immediately wrestled him into an affectionate
headlock. David tapped Tonka's huge bicep to request a
breath of air. He loosened his grip slightly.

'Cream always rises to the top lads. It's only a matter of
time before Steve Heighway hears the good word about yours
truly. Then it's Anfield and the Champions' League for me,
relegation battles and the Worthington Cup for you Toffees,'
David said happily.

'You'll regret that,' Tonka said calmly.

Luke crouched down on one knee so he could look David in the eyes. 'Do you have a torch?' he said.

At first, David stared back in confusion, but eventually he nodded his head as best he could.

'Meet us at Baker's Corner in an hour. Bring a torch, a sleeping bag, CDs and plenty of food,' Tonka said. He released the headlock and neatly dumped David onto the bonnet of his mother's cream Ford Fiesta.

'By the way. Tell your folks you're staying at my gaff tonight,' Luke said without looking back.

Tonka followed Luke out of the front garden. David climbed off the bonnet. He watched Luke and Tonka walk down Merrion Grove towards the laneway. Finally he called after them. 'Where are you going now?'

Tonka turned back to answer. 'Offy. Don't be late.'

David stood in his front garden watching the lads until they disappeared down the laneway. His head still felt a wee bit tender after four cans of Budweiser in the Music Centre. But this was a special occasion. It wasn't every day your dreams came true.

THE VENUE

Darkness had fallen by twenty past nine on Monday evening. Luke, Tonka and David were out on the town, celebrating. Armed with a battery-powered torch, portable CD player, three tubes of barbecue flavoured Pringles and eighteen cans of Budweiser, the boys made their way to the special venue to toast the good news.

'What a view,' Luke said quietly.

Tonka had picked the venue. He knew his way around Dalkey quarry and led the lads on a treacherous hike into the wilderness. Luke was apprehensive about a dangerous rock-climbing expedition, but wasn't too pushed to tell the lads about his fear of heights. Instead, he kept his mouth shut and said a little prayer. 'Please don't let me fall.'

God was on Luke's side. He made it to the summit and joined Tonka and David by the Air Safety beacon. This was an imposing white pole set in the centre of a massive square of concrete slabs fenced in on each side by metal railings. The pole jutted twenty feet into the air with a bright red bulb on top which flashed on and off at five second intervals. Tonka explained the beacon was a radio transmitter which helped to guide aeroplanes flying into Dublin. Set on the side of a cliff at the highest point of Killiney Head, the beacon gave a stunning panoramic viewpoint of the coastline from Killiney to Bray Head.

The boys climbed over the railings and stood on the concrete slabs. Each one quietly taking in his own view.

'Top notch venue, Tonk,' Luke said.

David sat down on a slab. He reached into his sports bag and opened a tube of Pringles. 'Luke,' he said. David held the tube up above his head. Luke reached in to take a handful while Tonka clicked the ring pull on a can of Budweiser. 'Children. Put away the sweeties,' he said. Tonka threw a can of Bud across to Luke. Then one to David. He ushered the lads to their feet with a wave of his giant left paw. Luke and David obeyed. The three boys stood together, forming a triangle. They held their cans high in the air. 'Here's to football and beer. The best summer ever,' Tonka said.

They clunked their cans together and swigged a mouthful. Luke kept a close eye on the progress of David. He was determined to swig longer than him. He had a reputation to uphold and it all depended on drinking. The last term of 3rd year in Woodlawn Comprehensive had been about nothing else.

Luke had had one previous experience of alcohol. He had stayed over at Ella's one Saturday in April when her folks went off to Manchester. They'd talked Isaac into buying some cans from the off-licence. He was reluctant to do so but eventually agreed and brought back ten cans of Heineken. Ella managed to drink four but ended up vomiting all through the night. Luke had drunk three and a bit before she began throwing up. He spent the rest of the night rubbing her back in the bathroom as she coughed, spluttered and groaned into the toilet bowl, then nursed her off to sleep. After the first mouthful on the beacon, a set of mind games began. David was a year younger than Luke and Tonka. But already he had managed four cans at the Temple Bar Music Centre.

Tonka was a different story. His birth certificate may have

said sixteen, but he would easily pass for nineteen or twenty. The night before he had drunk seven cans of Budweiser in the Music Centre and a pint at the bar. Not a bother to him. When Jerome drove in to collect Ella and the Funky Starfish, he was shocked to discover Tonka standing outside the stage door with an unconscious David Swayne draped over his shoulder.

The battle lines were clearly drawn. Luke had to drink more than David. Tonka was already the undisputed king of beer, but the positions of prince and court jester were still up for grabs.

Luke took another generous swig.

'You're in a hurry,' Tonka said stoically.

Luke glanced at him. 'Can't hack the pace?' he replied confidently.

Tonka chuckled quietly and watched Luke take another copious swig, just to stress his point emphatically. David wasn't buying into the hype. He was sipping his beer slowly, like someone forced to consume a can of grade-A plutonium. The virginal hangover he'd endured that very morning was more than enough to turn him off beer for life. But, as with most things, peer pressure conquers all.

'Imagine. We could be signing for Everton next week,' David said.

Luke wasn't so sure. 'It can't be that easy. The boss reckons there'll be a few trials.'

Tonka stood up. He sunk the remainder of his can. 'Trials, youth academy, pro contract. Easy as that.'

Luke and David laughed. Tonka took the flimsy green plastic bag from Grogans off-licence out of his sports bag and hung the handles from two separate branches of a nearby tree. He backed up ten yards or so and squashed his empty can into a little ball. Luke and David watched with intrigue as Tonka lobbed the can towards the bag. It went straight in. 'He shoots, he scores,' he screamed in celebration.

The tone for the evening had been set. Luke and David struggled on with their first can while Tonka broke open number two.

By half one in the morning David was fast asleep. He had managed four cans of Budweiser before feeling the pace. It had been a good night. The lads drank, danced about, had a few games of Bud-can basketball. But the main effect of alcohol on teenage boys is to loosen their tongues. Discussions had raged: the upcoming trial, how the other Enders would react to the news, Ille's surprise omission. But now that David was asleep, Luke and Tonka went on to more personal issues.

'Did you call her yet?' Tonka said.

Luke clicked the ring-pull on his fifth can. 'No,' he replied succinctly.

Tonka smiled as Luke started to slug. 'Why not?' he asked quietly.

Luke swallowed an unhealthy gulp of beer and then belched loudly. He attempted to focus on Tonka who sat on a muck mound ten yards away. The problem was, Luke could see no further than five feet in front of him. He was blatantly drunk, but like most teenage drinkers considered himself sober as a judge. Tonka decided to help Luke's desperate squinting search. He threw an empty Pringles tube at his head.

'Awoh,' Luke groaned.

'Over here,' Tonka said, waving his right hand.

Luke concentrated hard. He could see Tonka, but there were two sets of him. In the end, Luke closed his right eye and focused on the left hand side Tonka. 'Right . . . thing is,

I'm not calling her first. She's in the wrong, I'm in the right. End of story,' Luke said.

Tonka nodded his head in agreement. He took a casual swig of beer. Luke was very proud of his theory. He replayed it in his head, muttering self-congratulations.

'The thing is, Luke,' Tonka said. 'What if she doesn't call?'

Luke smiled. He stood up unsteadily and wobbled forward across the grassy verge below the concrete slabs, can in hand. 'She'll call,' he slurred into Tonka's face. Luke patted his friend on his enormous right shoulder and turned to walk back to the beacon. 'She'll definitely call,' he said confidently.

It was at this point that Luke stumbled on a loose rock and collapsed, face first, onto the grassy verge. Tonka was the last man standing, yet again. The majority of Luke's fifth can was dribbling down the hillside.

Tonka was in no hurry. He finished his can and took a successful three-point shot at the Bud-can basket before coming to Luke's aid. He was passed out on the verge, but at least he hadn't thrown up. Tonka lifted him up over his left shoulder and carried him up to the concrete slabs.

Minutes later, Luke had one last fleeting flash of consciousness. He focused on Tonka who was busy zipping up his sleeping bag. Luke smiled. 'She'll call,' he said sleepily. Tonka didn't reply. He lay Luke's sports bag beneath his head for a pillow and went off for a stroll about the quarry, can of Bud in hand.

The next morning Luke and David groaned awake around the same time. 'Unnhhh', 'urghh' and 'arggh' were the only sounds they could communicate with in the blistering morning sunshine.

Luke glanced about. Their first night of reckless teenage abandon had been rather civilised. All the beer cans and empty tubes of Pringles were safely tidied away in the green plastic bag from Grogans. They were lying in their sleeping bags on the grassy verge, beneath the cover of the concrete slabs.

'Where's Tonka?' David said weakly.

Luke mumbled something inaudible and shrugged his shoulders. He had a splitting headache. But that was the least of his worries. An icy cool liquid was gushing down his head, back and shoulders. 'Argggghhh!' Luke screamed. He rolled down the grassy verge in his sleeping bag in a desperate bid to avoid a further soaking. Tonka was standing on the concrete slabs above David's head. He wore a devious grin. 'Good morning, ladies,' he said.

Luke noticed the handle of a black bucket hanging from Tonka's right hand. David was zipped up tight in his sleeping bag. Escape was impossible. The only way to avoid a soaking was to beg for mercy and forgiveness.

'What did I do?' he pleaded.

Tonka considered this question carefully. 'Well, on the one hand, you did win a Cup Final by yourself,' he said. David smiled. He nodded his head enthusiastically. Surely this fact alone would save him from a soaking. But Tonka wasn't finished. If there was an 'on the one hand', logic dictated there must be an 'on the other hand'. 'But, on the other hand . . .' Tonka stalled to add suspense. '. . . you're a smart-arse Liverpool supporter.'

Luke couldn't bear to watch. Tonka tipped the contents of the bucket over David's head. The high-pitched scream of 'argghhhhh' spread across all of South County Dublin and most of Wicklow.

It was an evil thing to do. But David's cold shower was quite refreshing in the long run. Tuesday was a boiler of a day.

Twenty-six degrees. Tonka made the suggestion of a peace offering. While Luke and David settled on nearby Killiney beach, Tonka went home to fetch beach towels and a change of clothes for David. Naturally his new outfit included an Everton jersey.

'You'd better get used to it,' Tonka insisted.

Later that morning. Luke went off to the ice-cream van to buy three cans of Coke. While he stood at the back of the queue he had a chance to think about something other than the Everton trial. Ronald would nearly be home to Utrecht. Luke was still wearing the Dutch jersey. He rubbed the crest lovingly. No matter how Ronald felt, it was painfully obvious that his mother didn't feel the same. She really had 'moved on'.

Then, for no apparent reason, Luke thought about Ella. The argument outside the Music Centre seemed pretty low-key in the grand scheme of things. They argued that way a lot of the time. It didn't mean anything. They still loved each other. Then again, Luke would have said the same thing about Ronald and Martina a few days ago. That didn't stop an eighteen month relationship crumbling in a matter of days. Luke felt a cold shudder shoot down his spine. He imagined Weasel Adams and Ella, together. It wasn't a pretty picture.

'Three cans of Coke,' Luke said, having reached the top of the queue.

It was her fault though. Why should he bow down and come crawling back?

'One-eighty,' said the ice-cream man.

Luke handed him the money and took the three cans. 'Thanks,' he said blankly.

Luke walked back along the beach, weighing up his next move carefully. He realised how risky it could be, but was strongly inclined to try another bout of the silent treatment. After all, Martina had shuffled uncomfortably outside Gino's Café as Luke had shown his disapproval of Jonathan D'Argo with complete silence. Now it was Ella's turn to feel the freeze. Surely Jerome had mentioned news of the trial in the Barnes household. And Ella knew better than anyone, even Martina, what a momentous event a trial at Everton would be for Luke.

Whatever kind of fight or disagreement they were having, if Ella heard this news she would have to bite the bullet and call. If he meant anything to her, she would call. And Luke was pretty certain what he meant to Ella.

He arrived back at the spot Tonka and David had picked for sunbathing and bird-watching. He sat down beside David and handed out the cans of Coke. Jerome would accompany the lads to Liverpool in seven days time. Ella had until then to make her move. Luke wasn't concerned. He felt sure she was already hammering down the front door of 8 Montague Avenue, desperate for reconciliation. But he was in no rush to get home. The sun was shining and the radio was playing. No need to hurry.

One Last Chance

Ella didn't call at 8 Montague Avenue on Tuesday. Luke asked Mrs Hendy when he got home from Killiney. No one called all day. She didn't call on Wednesday, Thursday, Friday, Saturday or Sunday either.

It was now Monday evening, ten to seven. Luke sat on the couch in the living room reading a copy of Everton Monthly. He was within touching distance of the phone, just in case. Martina came out of her bedroom with an IT textbook beneath her right arm. 'Did you pack your bag?' she said brightly.

Luke didn't reply verbally. He simply pointed at the two large sports bags lying next to the living room door.

Martina nodded her head. 'Right,' she said softly.

Luke went back to an article about Gary Naysmith, the Toffees' young defender from Scotland. Martina was standing in front of him, looking his way. It was obvious she was waiting for an opportunity to break the ice. But she could whistle as far as Luke was concerned. The silent treatment would continue. Martina sighed sadly, realising that her punishment was set to continue. She walked to the coat rack in the corner.

'I'm going out. I'll see you later,' she said.

Luke didn't lift his head in the slightest. Before she departed Martina made one last attempt. 'Bye,' she said.

Luke flicked a page of Everton Monthly abrasively.

Martina cut her losses and left. When she shut the living room door behind her, Luke immediately took up his covert position by the bay window.

The silent treatment was one thing. But keeping tabs on her treacherous dealings with that slimy eco-snake Jonathan D'Argo was another. Luke monitored Martina walking up Montague Avenue, ready to curse the sight of D'Argo's flash Cherokee Jeep. Martina disappeared from view.

'Cow,' Luke said quietly.

Martina would consider this shortened insult as a sign of progress. Luke was still mad at her. But the venom was seeping out of his fury. Removal of the word 'stupid' from his catch phrase of abuse was quite an achievement. He sat down on the couch and stared at the phone. 'Come on,' he said desperately, urging the last-minute drring-drring of victory.

It was typical. Stubborn was a word and state of mind Luke Farrell knew a lot about. Nearly everyone in his life had a stubborn streak a mile long. Ella Barnes had one the length of the River Nile.

'And she calls me immature,' Luke snapped to the phone. Apart from the fact that he was now talking to an inanimate electrical appliance, Luke was thinking clearly. Maturity was the bone of contention here. Ella considered his attitude immature. It seemed to Luke that this theory was one of womankind's deadliest weapons in arguments with men. Logically, if Luke made the first move towards reconcilation then he would be acting maturely and he would have the advantage.

'I'll show her maturity,' Luke said to the phone. He jumped to his feet, grabbed his keys from the kitchen table and his white Nike tracksuit top from the coat rack. It was time to prove a point. The policy of the silent treatment had failed against Ella. But that didn't mean she'd won the fight.

Luke was about to employ subtlety, guile and unwavering patience. Qualities he would have to develop quickly.

Luke stood outside the porch door of 18 Sycamore Street. He rang the doorbell once. Mo Barnes appeared seconds later wearing a broad smile. 'Congratulations,' she swooned.

Luke smiled. Mo embraced him with a loving hug. Afterwards they went inside. 'I haven't seen you since the news,' Mo said as she and Luke walked down the hallway to the kitchen.

Jerome was sitting at the kitchen counter supping a bowl of oxtail soup. The sports pages of the *Daily Star* were spread across the table. 'What's the matter?' he said anxiously.

'Nothing,' Luke replied.

Jerome pointed his dripping spoon in Luke's direction and issued a stern warning. 'Early night tonight. I want you down the docks at half nine.'

Luke glanced at Mo in confusion. 'The docks?' he said.

Jerome thought about it momentarily. Luke grinned at Mo. He knew full well Jerome was referring to the ferry port. This cheek agitated his manager.

'The ferry place . . . you know,' he snapped. 'Don't be late.' Jerome went back to the newspaper and his oxtail soup. Mo opened the fridge door. 'Are you nervous, love?' she said.

'Yeah,' Luke replied quietly. He wore his cheeky schoolboy grin. Mo Barnes was like putty in his hands when he brought out those trademark dimples and talked in his posh, polite voice.

'You'll knock them sideways,' she said confidently. 'Would you like something to eat?'

'No thanks, Mrs B. I just called up to see Ella,' Luke said.

'She's not here,' Jerome replied immediately.

Luke looked at Mo for confirmation. She seemed surprised

such simple information was out of his reach. 'Did she not tell you? They're recording their demo tonight,' Mo stated.

Luke was stunned. He stood in the kitchen, dripping with anger and embarrassment. Mo continued to root in the fridge while she explained. It seemed Weasel Adams had booked four night-time sessions for Ella and the Funky Starfish in Output Studios off Dame Street. Mo was a hive of information. Apparently Weasel was sole heir to the Adams Nationwide Furniture Stores empire. He lived near Bono and Neil Jordan in the hills of Killiney, drove a 01-D, silver Cherokee Jeep, spoke three different languages fluently and was in the second year of a Law degree at Trinity College.

Spoken Word Management was a mere hobby but he had already signed Ella and the Funky Starfish to a twelve month contract. Luke couldn't bare to listen any more.

Looks, talent, money and a big jeep. What did Luke have? A weekly bus ticket.

'Are they in there now?' Luke said, cutting in on Mo.

'Yeah, eight till eight,' she replied.

'I'd better go.'

Luke didn't waste any time. He fled from 18 Sycamore Street without another word. He had to act quickly to save his girlfriend.

Sitting alone on a deserted 46A bound for the city centre, Luke could see things clearly at last. 'Smooth, Weasel, very smooth,' he muttered under his breath. Weasel Adams had no interest in the Funky Starfish or their music. The only thing he wanted to be attached to was Ella. Luke was sure of that, but Weasel was a cool customer. To achieve his aim he needed to surgically remove the boyfriend. Weasel had the money, time and resources to perform such a task, unless Luke foiled his devious scheme.

The 46A zoomed down Dawson Street. Luke gnawed away at what was left of his fingernails. Seven days of the silent treatment had backfired in a big way. This was the kind of opportunity predators like Weasel Adams craved. Ella had probably spent the whole week in his company. Even Mo swooned when she mentioned his name. Luke leapt from the 46A at the bus stop on Suffolk Street and sprinted up towards the International Bar on Exchequer Street. He was determined to fight it out. But Luke had a dull feeling in his chest that he might be too late to prevent Weasel making off with the prize. Either that or he was having a heart attack.

Luke stood outside the Mercantile Bar on Dame Street, waiting for a chance to cross the wide thoroughfare. A steady stream of cars zoomed round the corner from South George's Street, blocking his progress.

'Come on,' Luke said softly.

The traffic lights turned red and Luke saw an opening. He darted across the street. Now it was time to ask a geography question. Two attractive blonde women dressed up for a night's clubbing were walking towards Temple Bar. Luke plucked up the courage and stopped them. 'Excuse me,' he said politely.

The girls smiled. They were drop dead gorgeous but Luke knew their friendly expressions were part of an assessment which drew the conclusion, 'ahhh, isn't he cute?' rather than 'oahh, isn't he tasty?'

'Do you know where Output Studios are?' Luke asked.

The girls looked at one another. One pointed a slender finger back down Dame Street. 'Turn right after Apache Pizza. It's about four doors down.'

Luke smiled. 'Thanks,' he said.

The girls walked away. They may have considered him a

kid but it was always nice when someone so attractive smiled your way. It gave Luke a small injection of pride and positive spirit. He jogged down Dame Street, keeping an eye out for Apache Pizza. When he saw it up ahead, the picture became even clearer.

Luke stood on the pavement watching Weasel Adams, Ella and the Funky Starfish chow down. His bottom lip began to quiver. It was like an action replay of Gino's Café the week before. Isaac and the Starfish sat together at a table, sharing a sixteen-inch pepperoni pizza and a slender home-made cigarette. Ella and Weasel sat at a separate table. He kept smiling at her, constantly displaying those trusty pearly whites to emphasise his outrageous good looks. This kind of thing would eventually wear her down.

If it hadn't already.

Ella exuded the body language of an unscrupulous cat seeking out a tummy rub. She balanced her right elbow on the table and cradled her cheek on the palm of her hand. Weasel said something; she laughed. Weasel said something else, her eyes lit up like a Catherine Wheel. She laughed uncontrollably. So much so that she had to employ her left hand on his shoulder, in case she burst her sides.

'Stupid cow,' Luke hissed. He felt nauseous. A steady flow of pedestrians walked by. They looked and wondered why he had frozen to the spot, why his face was so pale? Was he a muddled mime act, trying to find a way back to Grafton Street?

Luke was well aware of the people staring. His midriff was a whirl of butterflies flying in formation. But his legs were paralysed. He couldn't bring himself to move. That same question popped back inside his head. 'Why is this happening?' Ronald was gone, Martina might as well be. And now Ella.

At that moment, Luke could have been knocked over by a gentle breeze. But not for long. The one thing Luke Farrell was sure of was his character. In footballing terms, Weasel had a three goal lead. But Luke would never quit. Weasel Adams had a fight on his hands.

A sudden strain of determination flowed through his veins. Luke managed to shuffle inside a nearby Centra and bought himself a Tuna Salad sandwich, a kingsize packet of Rancheros and a bottle of Coke. He walked back across Dame Street and settled down on a concrete litter bin at the bottom of South George's Street to watch Ella. When the Starfish party left Apache Pizza and headed back inside Output Studios, Luke would pay them a surprise visit.

FACE TO FACE WITH WEASEL

Luke barely touched his packet of crisps or his sandwich. He didn't feel much like eating. Thirty yards across the road his so-called girlfriend was enjoying an Apache Pizza of betrayal with Weasel Adams. Every time she laughed at his jokes or touched his arm in an over-familiar way, Luke had to turn away in disgust.

The Funky Starfish were the first to leave the pizza parlour. Weasel and Ella remained behind to pay the bill. Luke was ready to sprint across Dame Street, whatever colour the traffic lights, and smash Weasel's immaculate mug until he appeared somewhat less attractive. He took two deep breaths to calm down.

Ella and Weasel left Apache Pizza. They walked down a narrow side street and caught up with the Funky Starfish outside a building with a large blue door. Weasel came to the fore and pressed a button on the intercom. The door opened; when everyone was inside, Luke made his move. He calmly walked up to the traffic lights at the corner of South George's Street and pressed the pedestrian WAIT button. When the electronic beep-beep sounded, Luke skimmed across the road. He wasn't quite sure how to approach Output Studios. He needed a plausible excuse to explain his surprise visit. But that was a trivial matter. There was a much more important issue at hand. Winning back his girlfriend.

Twenty seconds later Luke arrived at the large blue door. Output Studios . . . It didn't look much from the outside. Just your run-of-the-mill three-storey building. He pressed the button on the intercom. Another electronic buzzing sound followed.

'Yeah,' a nondescript voice said.

'Erm. I'm here to see the Funky Starfish,' Luke replied.

A perpetual electronic hum rang out of the small rectangular speaker.

'Luke?' the voice finally said with surprise.

'Yeah,' Luke replied.

A different buzzer sounded. The blue door unlocked and Luke pushed it open. Stage one complete.

Luke locked the front door behind him. He stood in the hallway, drenched in darkness. The sound of footsteps pounding down the staircases above caught his attention. He braced himself for the arrival of Weasel.

'All right, stranger,' a familiar voice said. Isaac was standing at the top of the first staircase, illuminated by a shaft of fading daylight from a first floor window. 'Come on up,' he continued.

Luke started up the first staircase. Isaac waited for him to reach the top before they climbed the second two floors together. Isaac was in a bright and breezy mood. He explained how much work they'd done on 'Star Rider'. This was a song Isaac had written himself and the first track on their demo. 'Ella's inside,' he said as he opened the door to the studio control booth.

It was a large spacious room with two black leather couches facing one another and separated by a low-lying glass coffee table in the centre of the room. The walls and ceiling were covered with grey foam insulation and the floor with a thick shag pile carpet. At the far end of the room was a mixing desk the size of a full-length snooker table beneath which were various tape machines and small dark rectangular boxes, decorated with green, red and orange lights.

'Pretty smart, yeah?' Isaac said brightly.

'Yeah,' Luke replied aimlessly.

A large glass window above the mixing desk showed the recording booth beyond. Luke nodded his head to the other Starfish, Cedric, Gubby and Dan, who were seated on the two couches. The only other people in the room were at the mixing desk. Weasel was one; Luke assumed the other to be a sound engineer.

'Hey, Wes,' Isaac said. Wesley spun round. When he saw Luke he smiled and walked across to Isaac's side.

'This is Ella's boyfriend, Luke. Luke, this is Wesley, our manager.'

Weasel smiled. Luke wanted to smash in those precious pearly whites then and there. But this wasn't the same situation as Gino's Café. The silent treatment was too obvious. A more subtle mode of expressing his disdain was called for.

'It's a pleasure, Luke,' Weasel said politely.

'Yeah,' Luke replied.

There followed an impasse. But it was more of a blank moment of silence between virtual strangers than a tense stand-off. Luke sported an indifferent expression. But Weasel wasn't picking up the negative signals. He pointed over his shoulder to the mixing desk. 'Would you like the grand tour?' he said.

'I suppose so,' Luke replied.

Isaac gave Luke a friendly pat on the shoulder before moving off to the fridge to fish out another can of Carlsberg.

Luke followed Weasel over to the mixing desk and was introduced to Rob, the sound engineer, a chubby chap in his late twenties wearing white Reebok pumps, faded black Wranglers and a black Iron Maiden T-shirt beneath a tattered tartan shirt. He had countless stringy strands of long brown hair and wore Coke-bottle-bottom glasses.

Ella sat on a wooden stool in the sound booth. She held a lyric sheet in her hands and wore headphones over her ears. A bottle of Evian mineral water sat beneath the stool. She still hadn't noticed Luke.

Weasel looked at him with that hopelessly charming grin. 'Do you want a word with her?' he asked.

Luke didn't reply, but somehow managed to raise a pleasant smile. Weasel pressed a button on the mixing desk: 'Ella,' he said lyrically.

'What?' she replied without looking up.

'There's someone here to see you.' Weasel winked at Luke as if they were newly-established best mates. Luke took another deep breath and counted to twenty-five. Ella finally raised her eyes from the lyric sheet. This was the most important moment in their entire relationship. Luke traced her expression carefully. He was searching for clear-cut signs of guilt, shock and shame.

'Hi,' she said softly.

Ella wore a wide smile. Luke felt faint. They were still in the middle of an argument. The usual process for make-up was simple. After an argument, a cooling-off period ensued. When they finally saw one another again, Ella would wear a surly expression that could only be lifted by countless apologies or numerous failed attempts to raise a smile or a giggle. But this time Ella wasn't looking surly.

Ella came out of the sound booth and embraced Luke with a warm and loving hug. 'What are you doing here?' she asked. Luke felt cold. His worst fears had been realised. Ella's question was saturated in guilt. They looked at one another. Ella immediately sensed something was wrong.

'Ella. We're ready to go,' Rob said.

It seemed ironic that her blossoming career in music was yet again getting in the way of their relationship. She didn't move straight away. Instead she looked to Luke for advice.

'Go on,' he said coolly.

Ella kept a close eye on Luke as she moved back into the sound booth and prepared to sing the lead vocal on 'Star Rider'. Meanwhile, Isaac handed him a can of Carlsberg. He didn't feel much like drinking. But the sight of Weasel lounging in his swivel chair next to the mixing desk, smiling in at Ella changed his mind. Weasel had stolen his girlfriend; Luke might as well steal some of his beer.

It took six takes for an unusually indecisive Ella to nail the lead vocal on 'Star Rider'. Luke polished off two cans while he waited for the chance to confront her. It was a strange feeling. Having to stand there behind Weasel and listen to the symphonic voice he had helped to set free.

Isaac and the other Starfish sat back on the couches drinking cans of lager while reading a stack of magazines and newspapers. It seemed the only people taking an interest in Ella's performance were Weasel and Luke.

'Great stuff,' Weasel said after the sixth take. 'Nailed it babe.'

Luke shot Weasel an evil stare as he spun round from the mixing desk on his swivel chair. He took one last swig from his third can of Carlsberg before plonking it back on to the coffee table and marching into the sound booth. Ella was removing her headphones when Luke appeared inside and locked the booth door behind him. They stood still for a moment, studying each others faces carefully. All of a sudden Luke was lost for words. It was left to Ella to break the silence. 'How are you?' she said quietly. Such a mundane question was a helpful push-start. Luke decided to be sardonic with his reply. 'Not too bad. I'm off on a little trip tomorrow.'

Ella conceded the point. 'Yeah, Pop said,' she replied casually. 'Good luck.'

Luke could hardly believe it. Was this really the same girl? How could she comment on the most important two days of his life with a feeble and downright insulting 'good luck'. She had turned her back on him and was busy gathering together the lyric sheets for 'Star Rider'.

'Is that it?' Luke said. 'Good luck.'

Ella sighed; she picked up her bottle of Evian from beneath the stool and faced him. 'What do you want me to say?'

Luke laughed dramatically. 'When did you find out about the trial?' he asked sharply.

'Last Monday,' Ella replied.

'Seven days ago. And you couldn't even be bothered to phone me or call round,' he said.

She walked towards the door of the sound booth. She stopped beside Luke briefly and glanced his way to explain. 'I've been busy.'

Ella opened the door. Luke intervened, slamming it shut again. This violent thump drew the attention of Rob and Weasel. They stared through the glass window above the mixing desk anxiously.

'You've been busy,' Luke shouted angrily.

Ella wasn't impressed with his tone of voice. She pushed her lyric sheets into his chest roughly. 'Yes, I've been busy,' she said. 'The whole world doesn't stop and start for your stupid football career.'

Luke tried to interrupt with a vicious counter-attack but Ella stormed onwards. '. . . For your information, while you spent the week sulking like a four-year-old child, we've been working on a four-track EP. Wesley has the managing director of Sony International waiting on this demo. If he likes it, we're as good as signed. That's why I didn't call.'

It was a world-class explanation. Luke was reeling on the ropes, but Ella was too exhausted from the shouting match to finish him off. A short period of ceasefire was called for, but Luke still had a secret weapon up his sleeve.

'Are you sure it's about business and not pleasure?' he muttered.

'What?' Ella replied with a sense of genuine confusion.

Luke should have stopped talking then and there. But his mouth was working six steps ahead of his brain. He said it without thinking. A common design flaw with men. 'You and Wesley.'

Ella rolled her eyes to the heavens and groaned in disbelief. Luke felt she was patronising him. He stormed on with the accusation. 'Don't try to deny it. I saw you in Apache Pizza. You were all over him.'

Ella couldn't help herself. She burst out laughing. Her giddy cackle sounded like that of an elder sibling ridiculing a younger child for their innocent belief in Father Christmas. Luke felt a sharp shrinking of his ego. He wasn't impressed by her reaction and he lashed out. 'Stupid slut,' he said firmly.

Ella stopped laughing. For a moment there was silence, then there was sound. She swung a sturdy slap at Luke's face. The atmosphere in the sound booth had changed considerably. Luke touched his roaring red cheek with his fingertips. Ella drilled a toxic stare through him. 'Get out,' she said calmly.

With possibly the worst sense of timing in the history of the human race, Weasel popped his head through the sound booth door. He wore a charming smile, as per usual. 'Everything OK?' he asked softly.

Ella sustained her poisonous stare at Luke. But she replied to Weasel in a bright and cheerful voice. 'Yeah, Wesley, everything's fine. Luke was just leaving.'

Luke didn't kick up a fuss. There was no point in arguing. Ella had made her decision. He walked past Weasel into the control booth and wished the Funky Starfish good luck with the rest of the session.

'Give them Scousers hell,' Isaac said supportively as Luke walked into the hallway. It was a thoughtful gesture. Isaac wasn't stupid; he knew something was wrong. But he wasn't about to take sides. Instead he waved goodbye to Luke as he trundled down the staircase sadly. Night had fallen outside. Luke shut the front door behind him and tucked his hands into his jacket pockets. He sauntered slowly along Dame Street. The impact of Ella's slap to the face had knocked him into a daze. He felt a strange sensation of numbness. It was only when the 46A zoomed past RTE studios in Donnybrook that Luke realised he and Ella were in serious trouble. No one had said the actual words, 'I think we should split up,' but with three more days to consolidate his position, it seemed Weasel was in position to complete the switch from band manager to boyfriend.

Luke shuffled uncomfortably in his seat. He didn't have time to mope about thinking of Ella. He had a trial with Everton football club. The chance to fulfil a lifelong ambition. This was a time to concentrate on football. Nothing else mattered.

'Plenty more fish in the sea,' Luke muttered to himself.

The top deck of the 46A was deserted. But the one person who needed to hear such an awful cliché got the message loud and clear. Everton here we come.

THE START OF A LONG HARD JOURNEY

Luke stood at the stern of the Stena Seacat, staring down at Dun Laoghaire harbour below. Tonka, David and Jerome were in Beefy Bill's Café awaiting their early morning fry-up. It was twenty past ten and a dull grey, gloomy sky hung overhead. The sun had failed to appear for the first morning that whole summer. Luke sensed a bad omen.

A crackled announcement splurted out of the PA speaker behind him. The Seacat was departing. Luke wasn't giving in. He continued to scan the harbour below, certain Ella would appear at the last minute, waving frantically and screaming, 'I was wrong, you were right,' proclaiming her love, and begging him to phone as soon as he arrived in Liverpool. He had dreamed of such an unlikely reunion the night before. Surely that was an omen too.

A dense rumble vibrated beneath Luke's feet. The Seacat was beginning to motor. Slowly, it inched away from its moorings, out of the harbour entrance and on into the open sea of Dublin Bay. Luke still wasn't prepared to give in. He squinted hard at the fading harbour, searching frantically for a distant yell of 'Luke' and a set of waving arms.

'You'll be lucky,' Jerome said, his voice appearing from nowhere.

Luke spun around sharply. 'What do you mean?' he asked defensively.

'They didn't get home till after seven this morning. She

was fast asleep when I left,' Jerome replied. He had his arms folded across his chest. He stared at Luke with that unsympathetic expression. 'I told you so,' it said smugly. But he had. Jerome had taken Luke aside soon after he and Ella had got together. He'd summed up his daughter's volatile nature in one golden sentence. 'She's just like that model aeroplane of yours,' he'd explained bluntly. Spitfire said it all. But Luke was desperate to retain some sense of dignity and pride. 'What are you talking about? I came out here for some fresh air,' he said unconvincingly.

Luke moved past Jerome and sauntered into Beefy Bill's Café with his head held high.

Jerome grunted cynically. '"Fresh air" my Arsene Wenger,' he said before following Luke inside.

The journey from Dun Laoghaire to Holyhead on the Stena Seacat took ninety minutes. Jerome and the boys spent the first sixty-five sitting in Beefy Bill's Café enjoying a traditional English breakfast.

Afterwards Jerome took the boys into the TV lounge near the bow and went into serious mode. They sat facing him, awaiting a little chat he entitled, 'The start of a long, hard journey'.

'I knew this day would come for you three,' Jerome said. The boys didn't butt in, they remained silent and paid close attention. 'All this season, you three have stood out. Ille may be ready in a year or two. But you three, you've got a real chance to make it.' Luke glanced at Tonka and David with an optimistic smile. Jerome's face was void of emotion. He stared at Luke. 'Something funny?' he said.

Luke was confused. 'What?' he replied softly.

'Is something funny?' Jerome reaffirmed.

Tonka and David were equally baffled by the manager's

serious tone. Luke didn't know what to say. But Jerome wasn't looking for a reply. He rolled up the left leg of his tracksuit bottoms. The boys stared at a smooth scar, eight inches in length, running across his kneecap.

'Look and listen. This is professional football. One bad tackle can ruin your career in the space of ten seconds, BANG! . . . Game over,' Jerome said, ' . . . but that's just for starters.' He rolled the leg of his tracksuit bottoms back down. The boys stared at him in complete silence. They were afraid to exhale, let alone move. 'Forty, maybe fifty thousand other boys are getting a trial like you this summer. A thousand might get schoolboy forms. From a youth academy of forty, three a season get pro forms, maybe. First team football at a Premiership club? There'll be up to six other pros competing for your position. In the lower leagues: two or three. Maybe more with the Bosman rule.'

Jerome sat back. The boys were shell-shocked. Another crackling announcement came over the PA speaker. 'Docking in Holyhead in fifteen minutes,' the voice said.

Luke was beginning to wonder if it was worth their while going on to Liverpool. From what Jerome had just told them, they'd save themselves a lot of hassle by waiting for the next Seacat home. But the lecture wasn't finished. Jerome looked at the boys carefully, then leaned forward. 'Having said all that, I, personally, think all three of you can make a career in the professional game . . .' Luke had barely glanced over to Tonka and David when Jerome interrupted with a sharp '. . . BUT, I want you to remember what you're up against. Be realistic, don't live in some Roy of the Rovers fantasy world. Believe in your ability, always approach the game positively and don't be afraid to express yourself.'

Jerome stuck out his right hand. He glanced at David and

they shook hands. Then he glanced at Tonka; they shook hands. Finally he looked at Luke; they shook hands. Jerome got to his feet. 'Right then, let's go show these Scousers how to play football.' The boys watched their manager leave the TV lounge, somewhat awe-struck by the power of his lecture. None of them seemed able to stand up. Jerome had to stick his head back into the lounge to prompt the boys into action. 'Come on,' he said impatiently.

Eventually the boys stood up and followed him down to the car deck.

The journey to Liverpool took four long hours. Tonka slept like a baby in the back, using his tracksuit top as a makeshift pillow. David sat beside him, reading a copy of Alan Hansen's biography. Luke sat up front. His job was to change tapes on the car stereo. Jerome had rung him the Wednesday before the trip, asking him to make up a few compilation tapes from Jay's record collection, making sure to give pride of place to The Jam and The Clash. Luke had put together six hours of classic songs.

'Rock the Casbah' was blaring out of the speakers when Luke spotted a large blue road sign up ahead on the side of the motorway. 'LIVERPOOL – 8 MILES' it read. He felt a quiver of adrenaline flow through him. He gulped anxiously.

'Nearly there, lads,' Jerome said loudly. 'Give sleeping beauty a kick.' Jerome manoeuvred the car into the slip lane and proceeded off the motorway. Luke glanced back at David. His head was still stuck in his book. Tonka slept peacefully beside him. Was he the only one to feel nervous approaching Liverpool? Imagine him at the trial. Luke tried to fight off the feeling of excitement brewing in the pit of his stomach. In less than twenty-four hours he'd be competing with some of the best young players in England for a place at Everton's youth academy. He needed to be calm. Nervous footballers rarely give good performances.

TERRY CULSHAW'S HOUSE

Tonka was wide awake and David had stopped reading from Alan Hansen's biography when the car rolled past Anfield. All eyes were fixed on the imposing structure of the Kop Stand. David sprawled over Tonka and stuck his head out the window like an over-zealous puppy.

'There it is, lads. There it is,' he said happily.

Tonka wasn't impressed. Luke was, but he didn't show it. David's eyes were alive with joy. He turned to the Corolla's rear window and strained to keep an eye on the ground as it dwindled into the background.

Suddenly Luke and Tonka perked up. The car curved around the perimeter of Stanley Park and made its way towards Goodison. At this point, David resumed reading Alan Hansen's biography. This infuriated Tonka. He flung a bag of unopened crisps at the side of David's head. 'Here, show some respect,' he said sternly.

David drew a breath of courage. He waited for a few seconds before quietly picking up the bag and gently chucking it back in Tonka's general direction. He waited for a physical response, but it wasn't forthcoming.

Luke and Tonka stared out the side window like comatose zombies while the car zoomed past the main stand at Goodison Park. They turned their heads in near unison to capture every possible second of sight in the rear window. Jerome spoke for the first time since they'd entered Liverpool.

'We'll be at Terry's house in ten minutes,' he said. David nodded his head to Jerome as a polite means of acknowledgement. Luke and Tonka didn't move a muscle. They were still straining to steal a glimpse of Goodison Park as it passed further into the background. David observed this fanatical act of faith for a few seconds before tutting in derision. 'Sad,' he said softly, before turning a page in his book.

Tonka and Luke didn't reply. They were determined to stare at Goodison Park until their eyes watered under the strain.

Terry Culshaw was a beanpole centre-forward who'd spent five seasons at Man Utd during the eighties. He and Jerome had played together for twelve years. Through the A and B youth teams, they were reserves until they both signed pro forms on the same day in 1981. After Jerome's career ended in 1984 and he and Mo moved to Dublin, Terry kept in close contact. They phoned each other once a week without fail. Terry did go on to play three first team games for Man Utd. All were in the early rounds of the Milk Cup before leaving Old Trafford in 1987 to join Oldham Athletic. From there he went to Stoke City, Rotherham Utd and finally Wrexham. He'd played over four hundred league and cup games and scored one hundred and thirty-nine goals. After retiring in 1996, Terry had become a scout for Everton, the team he'd supported as a boy. He was now a member of the youth academy coaching staff and the chief accommodation officer.

'Here at last,' Jerome said with a strange sense of achievement.

It was twenty minutes since Goodison Park finally disappeared from view. The journey through Liverpool's suburban landscape had culminated in a picturesque housing estate called Albion Oaks. The boys almost collapsed out of the car on to the pavement. Each one was eager to stretch the stiffness of a five-hour car journey from their limbs. Luke noticed they were parked outside an enormous semi-detached house. It seemed to have an extra front bedroom window tacked on either side and two broad living rooms below. The large white front door set in the centre of this throng of windows opened from the inside.

A man and woman stepped out onto the doorstep, both sporting cheerful smiles. Luke recognised the man from Tolka Park and the day of the All-Ireland Cup Final. He was lamppost tall, thin, white, completely bald on top with long thick strands of brown hair dangling round the back and sides of his head. He assumed the woman was the man's wife. She was deceptively small. Her arms and legs appeared so long and slender. Maybe it was an effect created by her smooth sallow skin, set off by her long dark red hair which flowed down to the small of her back.

Luke looked across at Jerome. He was grinning happily.

'Barnes, you scoundrel,' Terry said in a thick Scouse accent.

Jerome edged forward into the front garden. He and Terry approached one another like two cagey WWF wrestlers waiting to lock-up. Jerome made a sudden jerk forward. He buried his head into Terry's midriff and hoisted him clean into the air, up on to his left shoulder.

Luke and the boys watched in amazement. Terry was a big bloke. But Jerome easily yanked him off his feet like a two-year-old toddler. The woman walked over to his side and slapped his back. 'Put him down, you big kid. Give me a hug,' she said in a pronounced Manchester accent.

Jerome returned Terry to his feet and swept the woman into the air. 'I'll pick a rose for my Rose,' he sang in a deep soulful voice.

Terry smiled. He noticed the lads lined up against the side of the car, watching the joyous reunion with a certain sense of confusion. He walked over to introduce himself. Luke, Tonka and David stood to attention like army privates meeting their drill instructor.

'All right, lads. I'm Terry,' he said.

One by one, Luke, Tonka and David shook his hand. Jerome and Rose Culshaw were talking in the front garden. Luke earwigged carefully, but could only make out snippets of the conversation. 'How's Mo?', 'How are the kids?' It was pretty standard fare.

'Luke Farrell,' Terry said sharply.

Luke turned his attention away from the front garden. He stared at Terry with a real sense of fear and respect.

'The next Francis Jeffers, or the first Luke Farrell?' Terry said with a friendly smile. Luke smiled back.

'Hopefully not the new Stuart Barlow,' Tonka whispered sarcastically.

Terry overheard the comment. He turned to Tonka. 'He did score twenty-five goals for Wigan two seasons back,' Terry said. 'With a bit more luck it might have been that way for the lad with Everton.' Tonka didn't know what to say. All he could manage was an apologetic nod of his head.

Terry moved on to David, who was determined to keep his mouth shut. He was a red outsider amidst a trio of Toffees. Terry studied him quietly. 'Congratulations kid,' he said finally. 'Not many players win a match by themselves.'

David blushed red. 'Thanks,' he replied modestly.

Terry patted David on the shoulder. He walked back into the front garden to rejoin Jerome and Rose. A sudden sense of jealousy came over Tonka. He nudged David in the ribs with his elbow. 'I won the final, all by myself,' Tonka said in a mousy, mocking voice. Luke couldn't help but laugh.

'Gentlemen,' Jerome interrupted loudly. The boys turned their attention to Jerome. He threw the car keys through the air. Luke caught them. 'Unpack the car,' he added.

The boys watched Jerome, Terry and Rose disappear inside the front door. They shared a communal sense of disgust. Then they looked at one another, silently discussing their options. Without a single word they decided the best thing to do was unpack the car.

Albion Oaks was a quiet and tranquil set of cul-de-sacs, reminiscent of Elliot Park, where Alan and Cecilia Giles lived. A scorching afternoon sun sizzled the arms, legs and necks of the three Enders. Tonka and David waited for Luke to unlock the back door. But before he could turn the key in the lock, there was a noise behind them.

The three boys turned to look. A wondrous sight filled their eyes, commanding complete attention. A teenage girl appeared from the front door. She was accompanied by a small German shepherd puppy on a red leash.

'Stacy. Don't go past the bandstand,' Terry's voice called from inside the house.

'Yeah, yeah,' Stacy replied in a wonderfully dry Scouse accent.

She was divine. A combination of the best bits Terry and Rose Culshaw had to offer. From her father she took height, a trim, slender physique and a set of sparkling green eyes. And from her mother, everything else. The face of a fragile porcelain princess, smooth sallow skin, long slender limbs and a mane of dark red hair. 'Come on, Ringo,' she said to the puppy.

Stacy walked past the car and down the pavement. Tonka gave her a lengthy stare, but his interest soon faded. She was a cracker. But beautiful women had to possess an ency-clopaedic knowledge of the Super Toffees and enjoy the music of Slayer, Anthrax and the Nine Inch Nails before he would get excited. Somehow Stacy didn't seem that sort of girl. Tonka got back to the business of unpacking the car. Luke and David didn't share his opinion of 'thanks, but no thanks.'

Stacy Culshaw's walk from Albion Oaks commanded as much, if not more, respect and fanatical attention as Anfield or Goodison Park. Tonka felt the need to intervene. He gave Luke, and then David, a firm flick on the earlobe with his right index finger. They both squealed in pain.

'Cars don't unpack themselves,' he said dryly.

Luke and David rubbed their earlobes. They took heed of Tonka's reprimand and started unpacking the car. But neither could shake one image from their mind. Stacy Culshaw.

THE FIRST TRIAL GAME

Jerome acted like an over-protective parent on Tuesday evening. He ordered the boys up to bed at ten o'clock. No late-night TV, no chance to ogle Stacy. What a spoilsport.

Luke lay awake until one in the morning. His mind was blazing with thoughts of Ella in Output Studios with Weasel Adams by her side. The stunning sight of Stacy Culshaw earlier that day was a real shock to the system. It was the first time in a year Luke had looked at another girl and thought, 'yeah'. He wasn't a monk. He still tuned into The Late Lick with Trevor Nelson on MTV each evening to see the latest video from The Honeyz and Destiny's Child. He still stored back issues of Loaded and FHM beneath his mattress. Staring at a page three girl in the *Sun* and commenting 'wow' was all right. It was just a bit of fun and fantasy. But when Luke saw Stacy standing on the doorstep, he actually considered the possibility of something more serious. As a result, he refused to look at her for the rest of the evening. He kept his eyes trained on his plate during dinner, and on the black and white photographs and newspaper clippings featuring Jerome and Terry which the boys were force-fed afterwards in the living room.

In complete contrast, David couldn't tear his gaze from the scarlet vision. He had clearly fallen head over heels. Tonka was indifferent to her presence. But Luke had a funny feeling every time she was in the same room. It felt like she was watching him. He considered his theory for a second. It was extremely arrogant. Luke turned on to his side to sleep.

'Why would she look at me twice?' he thought to himself.

Jerome, Terry and the boys sat down to breakfast at half past seven on Wednesday morning. The conversation was limited to another edition of Jerome's 'Tales of The Cliff' with special guest star Terry Culshaw. Luke, Tonka and David sat there quietly. No one needed to say it. Nerves were beginning to take hold. The steaming pile of toast sitting untouched on a silver platter in the centre of the kitchen table said it all. The sudden disappearance of a teenage boy's ravenous appetite was a good sign of nerves.

Jerome and Terry supped the drains of their teacups and stood up. 'I'd grab some of that toast, lads. You won't play well with nothing inside you,' Terry said wisely. Luke, Tonka and David looked at one another anxiously. Suddenly, six hands mauled the platter. Jerome and Terry laughed. They walked out of the kitchen, down the hall and opened the front door. 'When you're ready, chaps,' Jerome said.

Tonka led the way down the hall. They were each armed with two handfuls of toast. It was a comical sight for Rose and Stacy, who were sitting in the living room watching television.

'Good luck, lads,' Rose said supportively.

Luke stopped outside the ajar living room door. He nodded his head politely as a reply. He noticed Stacy was wearing skimpy white Everton shorts and a blue bikini top. She stared at him while sipping her tea. There was an energy and intensity in her glorious green eyes like the magnetic pulse or the tractor beam from the USS Enterprise. For a stunning milli-second, Luke seemed to be floating towards her.

'Luke,' Jerome said loudly from the front garden. His sharp roar cut through the hypnotic power of Stacy's stare. Luke scuttled through the front door and shut it tightly behind him. He was the last one inside the car. Next stop, Mosely Park.

It was half past eight when they pulled into Mosely Park. A bank of football pitches stretched out into the distance. It resembled the playing fields of St Anne's or the Phoenix Park, Luke thought. There had to be at least thirty pitches. The large Tarmac car park was crowded with people, cars and coaches. The noise level was chaotic and unnerving.

Luke, Tonka and David took their sports bags from the boot of the car. Terry waited behind them to explain what was happening. 'OK, lads. This is the situation. Everton scouts scour Britain, Ireland, Europe and South Africa all year long to find promising young players under the age of sixteen,' he said. 'Then we invite them to Merseyside for two days of trial matches in June or July.'

The boys nodded their heads, but the scale of the task was lost on them. Ever since the All-Ireland Cup Final, Jerome had insisted Terry make plain the odds of securing a place at the youth academy. Terry had been reluctant to do so, arguing that such a pessimistic warning would hamper the boys' ability to perform on the day. But Jerome was adamant that they should know the odds they were up against.

'Lads, the mathematics works something like this. Two thousand players are invited for the first trial . . .' Terry stopped dead. He honestly felt it unfair to continue. But Jerome nodded his head to spur him on. '. . . a hundred and fifty are invited back for a second trial.'

Luke, Tonka and David were very quiet. Already, without kicking a ball, the chances of them making it back for the second trial were thirteen to one. Put plainly, that meant playing better than every player on their team, plus three others.

Terry sighed sadly. 'All the best, lads,' he said with a deeply ironic tone of voice. He walked off to join a group of men dressed in identical blue tracksuits. They were standing at the head of a huge crowd.

'Excuse me. Can I have everyone's attention, please?' a voice said loudly.

Jerome and the boys turned to watch. The noise level of the massive crowd gradually dulled to a murmur. A man with a brown mop-top haircut and bushy moustache came to the fore. He had a clipboard in his hand and looked vaguely familiar to both Luke and Tonka.

'Hello. My name is Alan Harper. I'm the head of Everton's youth academy,' he said. 'Welcome to Mosely Park.'

Luke and Tonka glanced at one another. Alan Harper was a tough-tackling yet skilful left-back in the Stuart Pearce mould who had enjoyed two spells at Goodison Park during the late eighties and early nineties. He wasn't an all-time Toffee great, but ultimately he was the man they needed to impress if they wanted a place at the academy.

Luke, Tonka and David ran on to field twenty-four with nineteen other hopefuls. Terry Culshaw pulled a few strings with the administrator and managed to keep the trio on the same pitch, wearing the same colour bibs.

Jerome shouted words of encouragement from the line. Not that the lads could hear him. There were at least thirty other people standing along the length of the touchline screaming words of wisdom. A bank of unfamiliar faces in blue bibs surrounded Luke. It was a crazy situation. Eleven players, all in ruthless competition with one another, expected to play as a team. Luke glanced at the tall blond kid preparing to kick off with him in the centre-circle. He could almost smell the fear. His face was an unhealthy shade of white. Jerome's voice somehow squeezed through the chaotic cacophony. 'You're not Maradona,' he called.

Luke turned to Jerome and nodded his head in reply. It seemed an abstract remark. But then and there it made complete sense. Within five minutes, he saw why. The pace of the game was off the scale. Every player on the pitch, even those lads playing in defence, was desperate for the ball. They all wanted to go on forty-yard runs, beat every player on the pitch and smash in a wonder goal.

Luke had a quiet word with Tonka and David, imparting Jerome's advice. In accordance, they each played the match in an unselfish manner. It wouldn't become evident in the indiscriminate mania of the first half. But in the punishing heat of the morning sun, players would grow tired. The second half was the time to impress.

Luke was having a tidy game. He played in the hole behind the tall blond kid who acted as a target man up front. Whenever Luke got the ball, he looked up, picked a pass, and fired it off. It was too warm for energy-sapping solo runs.

Anyway, the red defence was accomplished. Both centre-halves were six foot or so and built like concrete walls. The other blue attackers attempted to dribble past them, but a mean shoulder charge or crunching challenge put paid to their bids for glory.

Luke kept it simple. As a result, he created a rake of clear-cut chances for his team-mates to score. The blond kid missed five chances alone. In fact, the only goal the blues scored came from the left boot of Tonka. He ran on to a sublime through-ball from Luke and chipped the goalkeeper from the edge of the penalty area. It capped a wonderful display. Tonka won every tackle in midfield. He was untouchable in the air and his passing was neat, crisp and precise.

David Swayne was having a nightmare. He was marking a small, speedy black kid, who proceeded to tear him asunder. The reds scored twice; both goals down to defensive blunders from David. The first was sloppy marking at a corner; a simple loss of concentration allowed David's man a free header. But the second was an absolute howler. A hopeful punt up field from the red right-back landed five yards outside the penalty area between David and his goalkeeper.

'Keepers,' the blue No.1 shouted.

David decided to ignore this call. He tried to trap the ball and turn. He didn't notice the black kid sniffing behind him. Jerome held in a miserable groan as David committed an act of defensive suicide.

The black kid swooped in like a bird of prey and pinched the ball off David's left boot. He dribbled past the helpless goalkeeper and slotted the ball into the empty net. It was a winning goal for the reds in the last minute. The referee blew the final whistle soon afterwards.

Luke, Tonka and David walked back to the dressing rooms in silence. What could they say? None of them could remember David playing so poorly. There was still the second game on Thursday evening. But a dark thought lurked at the back of everyone's mind. David had blown his chance.

DISCO DROWNING SORROWS

It wasn't complete and utter silence on the car journey from Mosely Park to Albion Oaks. Luke's mix tape played artists as diverse as Bill Withers and Dr Feelgood while Terry made an occasional aside to Jerome. But in the back seat, Luke, Tonka and David were mute.

David stared out the window at the city streets passing by. Luke felt so sorry for him. He knew how passionately David felt about football. He hated making mistakes and would crucify himself over every sloppy pass or mis-timed tackle. This obsessive self-criticism was part of the reason David was a such a good player. He was never satisfied with a performance and set the target of perfection at the outset of each game he played in. He was always disappointed if he fell short of his target.

Today he fell a long way short.

'OK, lads,' Terry said as Jerome parked the car outside his front garden. 'Lunch, then a trip into town.'

Luke and Tonka managed to raise a smile between them. But it wasn't easy.

'Thanks,' Luke said, not wanting to seem completely ungrateful.

Jerome glanced at David anxiously. Before he could speak, Terry tipped him on the shoulder and urged him to come inside with a silent facial expression. 'See you inside, lads,' Terry said quietly.

Luke opened the boot of the car. He and Tonka took out their sports bags. David wrenched his own bag free from the boot and slammed the back door shut. Something needed to be said.

'Look, David . . .' Luke started feebly.

David didn't hang about to listen to words of consolation. He was well on his way across the driveway with his head hung low. He was so upset, he didn't notice Stacy and Ringo coming out the front door.

'Uh-oh,' Stacy said as he bumped into her. David retreated sharply. His face was white with terror.

'S-s-sorry . . .' he mumbled.

Stacy adjusted her grip on Ringo's leash. She smiled. 'Its OK,' she said kindly.

Luke and Tonka walked across and stood either side of David, just in case he fainted with embarrassment. Stacy smiled at all three of them. She was wearing a tiny pair of purple spandex hot pants and matching belly top. Her navel was pierced with a silver ball-bearing. A pair of sunglasses sat seductively in the hair on top of her head.

'How did the trial go?' she asked, not realising what a touchy subject it had become.

'Em, it was OK,' Tonka replied diplomatically.

Luke noticed how anxious Ringo was to leave. He began to whine and jump forward energetically. He longed to scamper about the spacious fields of nearby Albion Park. But Stacy was in the middle of a conversation. She would not be pressurised by an impatient puppy. A firm tug on his leash redressed the balance. Ringo yelped sharply. Then sat down obediently.

'Have you a match tomorrow morning?' Stacy said.

The boys looked at one another for a moment in consultation. Luke assumed the role of spokesman. 'No, not till six o'clock in the evening,' he replied.

Stacy fixed her stare on him alone. This was obvious. Luke returned the compliment. Even this innocent gesture felt like cheating on Ella. But he couldn't help himself.

'I'm going to the Vortex tonight,' Stacy said. 'Would you like to come?'

David replied yes instantly. Tonka nodded his head soon afterwards. But Luke had a funny feeling her invitation was aimed solely at him. It seemed like hours before Stacy broke her hypnotic spell.

'Come on, Ringo,' she said, glancing down at her faithful puppy. Stacy tugged the leash and led Ringo out on to the pavement. 'See you later,' she said.

The boys waved but were unable to speak. They watched Stacy take long measured strides along the pavement while Ringo struggled to sprint in front of her, beyond the constraints of his leash. This time, even Tonka had to stare longingly. She was magnificent; sporting the poise and sophistication of a cat-woman type super-villainess coupled with the wholesome charm of an intelligent super-model.

Stacy disappeared from view, but still the boys could not bring themselves to move until . . .

'Oi,' Jerome said loudly.

The boys turned to face him. He filled the front door with his massive frame. It was a simple case of 'don't even think about it'. Jerome pointed his thumb over his shoulder. Tonka and David hurried past him and up the staircase. Luke tried to follow suit but Jerome collared him in the hall. 'Especially you,' he said in a sinister tone.

Luke didn't protest. Jerome could have been standing on the doorstep for any length of time. The boys would still be frozen to the same spot if he hadn't spoken. There was a proper time and place to ogle Stacy Culshaw. It wasn't in her father's front garden. The Vortex later that evening seemed a much more appropriate venue.

Jerome and the boys spent the afternoon in Liverpool city centre. Terry thought a guided tour of the Albert Dock and a visit to the Beatles Museum would be a pleasant way to pass a few hours.

He was wrong.

The two places left off his list of attractions were the only places Luke, Tonka and David wanted to visit. Anfield and Goodison Park seemed a million miles away as Terry dragged them round the Liver Bird building. It was glorious summer's day, the perfect setting to wander on to the hallowed turf of Goodison Park or Anfield for the first time. A chance to inhale the stench of victory, tradition and pure footballing passion. Tonka smiled. Even the thought of it excited him. But instead, they wandered around the maritime museum staring at black and white photographs and model ships encased in glass cabinets.

When Terry called time on his 'fun day out', Luke, Tonka, David and even Jerome blew a communal sigh of relief. Each one started to look forward to the evening for different reasons. The lads would get to stare at Stacy for a few hours. Meanwhile, Jerome and Terry planned a quick trip down the M62 to visit Clark Gable's in Salford. The watering hole of their youth.

The boys began preparations for their night at the Vortex shortly after seven o'clock. Terry advised them to use the bathroom early in the evening to avoid Stacy. She was renowned for causing two-hour blockages. They each took a shower, and in Tonka's case a shave, before returning to the large guest bedroom.

David seemed to perk up considerably as he picked out a top to wear with his dark blue Levi's jeans. Luke turned the volume up on the Sanyo stereo, which stood on the windowsill. Another of his mix tapes was playing. David started clicking his fingers in time with the music. He began to sing along with Smokey Robinson and the Miracles on 'Tracks Of My Tears'. His hairbrush magically morphed into a microphone. He closed his eyes and sang along with gusto. 'People say I'm the life of the party, 'cause I tell a joke or two,' he squeaked.

Luke glanced across at Tonka who sat on his bed with his head buried in a copy of *Heavy Metal World*. He raised an eyebrow briefly at the amazing transformation but quickly returned to his magazine. Luke smiled. Gently, he lifted Tonka's bottle of cK one from the bedside table and squirted at David's left ear.

'Arggh,' David screamed in shock.

Luke began another infamous impersonation. He squawked along with Smokey, closing his eyes and using the cK one bottle as a microphone. David watched and listened to the wholly unflattering impersonation for a while before he decided to attack.

'You're dead, Farrell,' he said with phony malice. David rugby-tackled Luke in the midriff. They both fell to the floor. They began to wrestle for control of the cK one bottle. Tonka noticed the fracas below him. He yelled loudly. 'Here, that's not a bleedin' water-pistol.'

The struggle became a three-way affair. Tonka dived into the middle and quickly separated David and Luke with a moderate display of his dazzling strength. They both let out high-pitched squeals of pain. Tonka had taken hold of two earlobes. 'Now, listen carefully,' he said calmly. 'Return the bottle to the table.'

Tonka, Luke and David stood up together in a slow choreographed motion. Luke carefully placed the bottle of cK one back on to the bedside table.

'Thank you,' Tonka said.

He released his dual grip. David and Luke fell on to the floor with hefty sighs of relief. Both rubbed their throbbing ruby-red earlobes. Tonka sat back down on his bed and resumed his session with *Heavy Metal World*.

'Oh boys,' Stacy said in a clear, crisp voice. Luke, Tonka and David looked up at the bedroom door. Stacy stood there in a pair of knee-high purple suede boots and a mirror-ball mini-dress that stopped abruptly at the top end of her thighs. How long had she been standing there? No one was quite sure. 'I'm ready when you are,' she said softly.

Despite its glamorous title, the Vortex was in fact the downstairs lounge of McPhersons, the local pub, and a five-minute walk from Albion Oaks. Wednesday night was the under-eighteens' mineral bar disco, eight till twelve o'clock. Beforehand, Stacy and the boys went to Archie's Offy next door and bought twenty bottles of Hooch.

The next stop on the magical mystery tour was Albion Park. This was where the local teenagers gathered in and around the bandstand before the Vortex each Wednesday night to drink beer, vodka and alco-pops. It was a bright, sunny evening and countless drinking circles covered the football pitches of Albion Park. Luke, Tonka and David sat on the steps of the bandstand surveying the huge crowd below. Stacy had abandoned them for a while to do the rounds with her extended group of friends. She moved from circle to circle, receiving a warm welcome by all and sundry. It was obvious . . .

'The most popular girl in school,' Tonka said sarcastically. 'Now where have I seen that before?' he added.

Luke and David remained silent. Both knew Tonka was comparing Stacy to Cecilia Giles, the twin sister of Alan Giles and reigning femme fatale of Woodlawn Comprehensive. The similarities between Stacy and Cecilia were striking. Both were socialites, in love with their appearance and pushing self-confidence into the realm of delusion.

Luke and David were well aware that Tonka's jibe was a clear warning, but both were still under the hypnotic spell of those achingly beautiful green eyes.

An hour later, Luke, Tonka and David stood by the bar in the Vortex watching Stacy do her thing on the dance floor. Every male in the place seemed to swarm round her, desperate for a chance to stake their claim. Stacy seemed more interested in the music.

'I'm going for it,' David said nervously.

Luke smiled and laughed to himself. He glanced at David who sunk another can of Coke. David had finished four bottles of Hooch in Albion Park and was probably drunk enough to try it on with Stacy, but that was the fifth time he'd announced his intention to go for it. And, predictably enough, just as his legs began to carry him forward, David stalled mid-stride. Nerves had again got the better of him. He turned sharply to face Luke. 'I need the toilet. When I get back, then I'm going for it,' he announced confidently.

Luke nodded his head. He watched David wander off through the packed bar unsteadily. It was too good an opportunity to miss. 'David,' Luke shouted loudly. He caught David's attention. He turned round. 'Remember to wash your hands,' Luke said, breaking into a smug smile.

David gave him a one-finger salute before returning to the

task at hand. Luke smiled and kept a close eye on his unsteady progress a little while longer, just in case he bumped into some surly Scouse kid and things got ugly.

When Luke eventually turned his attention back to the bar he noticed Tonka had transported himself to a nearby booth with some girl who had long, jet-black hair and snow-white make-up. It seemed a simple case of boy meets Goth.

Standing on his own, sipping a can of Coke, Luke couldn't help thinking about Output Studios and Ella and Weasel spending another eight hours together in a confined space. It probably wouldn't take a lot longer for her to fall madly in love with the handsome swine.

Come to think of it, Weasel was probably rubbing his hands together with glee on Monday night while Luke committed romantic suicide. He suddenly felt a blanket of depression cover his head and shoulders. He had helped Weasel steal away his girlfriend. Luke needed a drink, something stronger than Coke.

'Hi,' a voice said from behind. Luke felt a hand pressed intimately against the side of his ribcage; Stacy's hand. He pulled away from her sharply, as if she were an opposing defender, but turned to face her in the same motion. She smiled at him while lifting the can of Coke from his hand. He watched her finish it off in one long, steady gulp. She threw the empty can on to a nearby table. 'Do you fancy a dance?' Stacy said brightly.

Luke shook his head. 'I'm not much of a dancer.'

His answer didn't matter in the slightest. Stacy took him by the hand and led him on to the centre of the dance floor. 'Livin' La Vida Loca' blared from the speakers. A crowd of envious lads watched as Stacy danced sexy Latino style with Luke. She had made her choice for the evening and no one else would get a look in. All the boys in the Vortex knew this, but one boy knew it more than the others.

Luke danced opposite Stacy for forty minutes. The music was atrocious; Backstreet Boys, 5ive, Steps and Robbie Williams dominating the play list. He spent most of the time looking for an excuse to sit back down. But Stacy was having none of it. Every time he pleaded for release, she'd pull him in closer.

Eventually Luke managed to escape to the toilets. He didn't need the facilities and satisfied himself with a quick wash and scrub of his hands. When he came out of the Gents, he scanned the interior of the club for Tonka or David. Tonka was nowhere to be seen. But Luke located David at the far end of the bar, standing alone. A small group of girls stood nearby at the cigarette machine. Each one stared at David with obvious intent. Luke decided to study from afar. The girls whispered to one another, smiled at him, two even walked up to ask him for the time. But David seemed completely unaware of his popular appeal. He just stood there, sadly sipping a can of Coke.

'Picky sod,' Luke exclaimed. He walked over to have a quiet word and approached David from his blind side. 'What's your problem?' Luke said firmly.

David spun round sharply and stared at him with a fierce expression of contempt. Obviously he wasn't in a very good mood. Luke quickly concluded that his horrific performance on pitch twenty-four in Mosely Park earlier that day was getting him down. 'Look, forget about it. There's still tomorrow. You'll make it up, no problem,' he said brightly.

David didn't bother to look Luke in the eye. He kept his head bowed low and shrugged his shoulders. Luke was still determined to cheer him up. He turned his attention to the small group of girls standing nearby and deliberated over

David's perfect match. It had to be the tall blonde nearest the dance floor. She was extremely pretty with a sexy beauty spot on her right cheek, above her upper lip. She was wearing cream combats, white Nike trainers and a tight army combat T-shirt. She would check on David every ten seconds or so, glancing his way, hoping for a split-second of eye contact. Luke stared across and quickly caught her attention. He subtly tipped his head in David's direction. At first, she was reluctant to reply, but Luke maintained his stare and eventually drew an emphatic nod of her head. Luke grabbed David roughly by the arm.

'What?' David snapped moodily.

Luke turned him away from the girls. He winked his left eyelid and grinned happily. 'You're in. Tall blonde in the cream combats,' Luke said.

David stared at him, his upper lip quivering. 'I didn't ask for your charity,' he replied dismally.

Luke was completely gobsmacked. He watched David walk off towards the fire exit. 'David,' he said loudly.

There was no reply. Luke turned to the tall blonde. She had been made to watch David spectacularly spurn her bashful advance. Now she felt an awful sense of disappointment and rejection. Luke was baffled by David's indifference. He turned to watch him weave his way through the crowd. Before he reached the door, Tonka appeared from nowhere to stop him. He said something in his ear. David shook his head. Tonka said something else; David shook his head again. He continued on out of the Vortex.

Luke made his way across to confer with Tonka. 'What's wrong with him?' he said loudly.

Tonka stared at Luke cynically. Apparently, his question had an obvious answer.

'What, what is it?' Luke demanded.

Tonka leaned into his left ear. 'He's just sore about you and Stacy,' he replied.

'ME and Stacy?' Luke said in disbelief. 'There is no me and Stacy.' He was emphatic on this point. Stacy was beyond compare. But when he ogled her, it was an exercise in window-shopping. Luke knew there were certain things in life you just could not get away with. Cheating on Ella with Stacy would be like buying a double-barrelled shotgun, loading it with ammo and handing it to Jerome.

'So, that's it, he wants Stacy?' Luke said.

Tonka nodded. A moment of silent contemplation was strangled by the distorted wail of Hear'Say's Oasis rip-off. Luke smiled, he had a brilliant idea.

'Go get the moody sod. I'll have a word with Stacy; set it up.'

Tonka sighed, he wasn't so sure. Luke tapped his bulging right bicep. 'Trust me,' he said.

Luke didn't have to search long and hard for Stacy. He simply headed for the largest mass of male bodies on the dance floor. Stacy was inside the ring of hormones, surrounded by a tightly-packed crowd jostling for position. Luke fought his way through to her side and leaned into her right ear.

'I need a word,' he said.

Stacy smiled. She took hold of his hand and followed Luke to the side of the dance floor. He smiled at her and took a deep breath before beginning his David Swayne sales pitch.

'What do you think of David?' Luke said.

'Why?' Stacy replied.

Suddenly the dance floor erupted with a huge cheer. The DJ was playing the Indie anthem 'Why Does It Always Rain On Me?' by Travis. The crowd swayed and sang in near unison. Luke had to lean into Stacy's ear again. 'He really fancies you,' he said.

Luke awaited her reply. But Stacy said nothing. She just stared into his eyes. It felt like the most exquisite bullet breaching the skin of his breast, plunging through the centre of his heart. Luke got the feeling this situation would be far from straightforward. Stacy took him by the hand and led him off the dancefloor, past the cigarette machine and out through the fire-escape.

When the chilly night air hit his face, Luke asked a single question. 'Where are we going?' he said softly.

Stacy didn't reply. But Luke couldn't stop himself from following her. He thought of David. He thought of Jerome, he thought of Ella. None of it mattered. Stacy had a quiet quality, a bewitching calmness that rendered him helpless. He would have walked to London if she led the way.

Albion Park was deserted and drawn in darkness. Luke and Stacy stood opposite one another on the granite floor beneath the hexagonal roof of the bandstand. They had been there for three or four minutes but neither had said a word. Luke wanted to, but nothing made sense. After all, what had they done wrong? He shuffled uncomfortably. A deep-rooted sense of guilt was giving him itchy feet. He knew his very presence beneath the bandstand with her was wrong. He had to say something. 'So, do you fancy David?'

It did seem like a stupid thing to say. But in reality, it cut right to the chase. Stacy took three careful steps forward. She smiled at Luke. 'No, I don't fancy David,' she said softly.

Luke stood breathless while she advanced, slowly moving her head to the side. He closed his eyes and allowed their lips to touch together. He could taste the faint remnants of orange lip-balm.

Now they began to kiss properly and he allowed himself to enjoy the soft, supple sensation of the kiss. Stacy caressed his face. She ran her fingers through his hair. Luke moved his arms round the small of her back. He allowed his fingers to trace the contours of her lean body, her navel, the base of her breasts, the indentations of her narrow hips. At that moment, nobody could convince him his actions were wrong.

But then Stacy touched his right wrist. Luke jerked back suddenly. He looked down at the friendship bracelet and then up at Stacy shamefully. 'I can't do this,' he said. He walked off, and sat down on the top step of the bandstand. Stacy waited for a while before she followed. She sat down on the same step, but a respectable distance away from him. Luke held his right wrist with his left hand. Stacy noticed a multi-coloured thread bracelet in the bright moonlight.

'What's that?' she asked.

Luke plucked up the courage to face her. 'It's a friendship bracelet,' he said softly. 'My girlfriend got it for me.'

Stacy nodded her head. They sat beside one another in silence for a while. Luke trained his eyes on the granite step beneath his feet. He was desperate to escape the symbolic err of Albion Park and get back inside the Vortex. If she stared at him again with those enchanting green eyes, there was no telling what might happen.

'You must really like Ella,' Stacy said.

At first, Luke couldn't believe his ears. Perhaps he was hearing things, the trick of a guilty conscience. But when he turned to Stacy, there was nothing but sincerity in her eyes.

'You, you know her?' he said reluctantly.

Stacy stood up and walked down the steps with the poise and grace of a finalist in a beauty pageant. When she reached the path below she turned to face Luke, illuminated by the bright moonlight overhead. 'Not really. We went on holiday to Majorca ten years ago. I haven't seen her since.'

Luke felt foolish. It was obvious Ella knew about Stacy and vice versa. Terry and Jerome had been best mates for twenty years. They kept in close contact.

'How long have you been together?' Stacy asked.

'Erm, a year,' Luke replied.

Stacy climbed back on to the fourth step and looked down at Luke. He was careful not to stare straight into her eyes. Even now, after the truth had come out, he still felt a reckless, uncontrollable desire for her. As if she had some secret pull over him. 'What a pity,' she said.

Luke was on his feet in a flash. 'We should head back,' he said weakly.

Stacy didn't reply. She had her arms folded across her chest, thinking out her next move. It brought home to Luke how pathetic men could be. If Stacy really had her heart set on kissing him again, he was hers, without question. He caressed the friendship bracelet, hoping to muster some mystical powers of Ella to defend him from Stacy's irresistible onslaught.

'Yeah,' she replied finally.

'No hard feelings?'

Stacy held her arms out wide. She wanted a hug. Luke let out a huge sigh of relief and accepted the invitation. As they embraced, he contemplated the right time to separate without appearing nervous, hasty or rude. This hesitation allowed Stacy an opportunity to run her fingers through his hair. Luke gulped quietly, realising she had enticed him back into her web. When they finally separated, he was powerless to resist another advance. Stacy stared at him, poised to strike. But just when all hope was gone, she showed mercy.

'Come on,' she said softly, holding out her hand.

Luke smiled, knowing full well she had let him off the hook. But deep inside he felt an unwholesome sense of disappointment. They walked from the bandstand hand in hand. But as friends. Luke knew this, but what conclusion would David and Tonka draw? When he and Stacy approached the entrance to the Vortex together, Tonka and David were standing outside, slugging bottles of Hooch.

The sight of Luke and Stacy together was enough for David. He stared at them briefly, then handed his unfinished bottle to Tonka and walked away.

'Oh no,' Luke said with a groan.

'He'll live,' Stacy replied coldly. She walked back into the Vortex to make the most of the final half-hour of music. Luke was afraid to face Tonka. When he eventually plucked up the courage to do so, Tonka shook his head with obvious disappointment. He slugged back his own, then David's bottle of Hooch and walked off.

'It's not like that,' Luke shouted.

Tonka kept walking. That said it all.

The next morning, Luke took every conceivable opportunity to insist nothing had happened between him and Stacy. Unfortunately the facts were against him. They had both been missing for twenty-five long minutes. David already had his suspicions; this mysterious absence had simply confirmed them. Relations between the two were strained to say the least. Tonka was handed the unwanted post of piggy in the middle.

Luke's mind was awash with worry. If this information was leaked to certain parties, i.e. Jerome, it could hammer the final nail in the coffin of 'Luke & Ella'. He might also find himself swimming home across the Irish Sea.

THE SECOND DAY

Tonka sat in the middle in the back of the car on the journey to Mosely Park. The only words David had said to Luke all day were, 'I don't want to talk about it. I'm more concerned with the trial.' Fair enough.

'Eton Rifles' played on the car stereo. Jerome noticed the pensive nature of his players in the rear view mirror. He offered them a stern warning. 'I hope you lot weren't drinking last night.'

No one bothered to reply.

'If you've blown your big chance for the sake of a night on the ale, chasing skirt . . .' Jerome was so incensed he couldn't finish his sentence. He just tutted in disgust. The boys paid no attention. After all, Mr 'Football-before-alcohol' had fallen into Terry Culshaw's house at half three that same morning singing 'That's Entertainment' at the top of his lungs. He and Terry had been drinking in some Manc pub till half two that morning, retelling tales of glory from the Cliff with the Stretford End faithful. If that wasn't bad enough, when they arrived back in Albion Oaks, Jerome had stumbled into the lads' bedroom to tell them how much he loved them and the Stretford Enders. He'd insisted they join him in a rendition of 'You'll Never Walk Alone'. Luke had pointed out that was Liverpool's anthem. At first Jerome seemed confused. But then he mumbled, 'Scousers aren't all bad' before stumbling out of the bedroom.

Mosely Park was again packed with cars, coaches and a swollen mass of bodies. Terry went off to join the youth academy coaching staff while Jerome led the boys down to the dressing rooms.

'Today's top tip . . .' he said as they walked. 'Individuals are the icing on the cake.'

David gave Luke a stern glance. He seemed to be emphasising Jerome's comment as an appropriate metaphor for his betrayal. Luke couldn't see how it applied. But then again, everybody in his life at the moment took any available opportunity to call him the bad guy.

There was a completely different atmosphere for the second day of trials. The noise level on the touchline had dropped off considerably, so too had the pace of the games. Luke, Tonka and David played with the red bibs on pitch fifteen. The game wasn't as scrappy and frantic as Wednesday's and Luke had the chance to impose himself going forward. It was still about the simple things. Passing the ball to feet, looking to create chances for his team-mates with incisive through-balls. But the blue defence was nowhere near as strong as the one they faced on Wednesday. Luke took full advantage of some lackadaisical marking and scored a stunning hat-trick. The first goal came out of nothing. The red right-back hit a fifty yard cross-field ball from inside his own half. Luke controlled the ball on his thigh ten yards outside the blue penalty area. In the same action, he wrong-footed his marker with a drop of the shoulder and drove at a back-pedalling defence. When he reached the penalty area, he skipped outside a flailing lunge by the blue left-back before smashing a scorching low drive across the goalkeeper into the bottom right-hand corner.

The second goal involved Tonka. He was playing out of his

skin. But everything he did was so simple and effective no one seemed to notice. After winning a block tackle in the centre-circle, he swept the ball out wide to the red right-winger. Tonka charged onwards to receive a neat one-two. Again, the blues were scrambling backwards. Tonka had an opportunity to drive into the penalty area and try a shot. But Luke had dragged his marker out to the edge of the penalty area and prepared to spin him. Tonka knew exactly what to do. He chipped a delicate cross over the heads of the blue defence. Luke left his marker for dead and arrived onto Tonka's ball to volley past the helpless goalkeeper.

The third goal was about opportunism. Luke worked tirelessly throughout the game. He chased the blue back four every time they got the ball and eventually got his reward. A sloppy lay-off from a blue centre-half to the right-back gave Luke a chance to nip in ahead of him. It wasn't a clear-cut opportunity. Once he'd stolen the ball from the right-back, Luke had to dribble past the two blue centre-halves and the goalkeeper before poking the ball into an empty net. This flash of something special drew a round of applause from the partisan crowd.

Luke stole the headlines. But David Swayne was the backbone of the victory. He turned in the sort of sterling performance that had won the All-Ireland Cup Final single-handed. The blue forwards never got a sniff. But apart from breaking down their attacks, David was driving forward from the back with the ball at his feet, distributing it to his midfield with the neat efficient accuracy of his heroes, Hansen, Rikjaard and Baresi.

When the referee blew the final whistle, Jerome was smiling. He gave the lads a thumbs up. Tonka and David met in the centre-circle. They shook hands and shared a laugh. Luke stood in the opposition's penalty area, shaking hands with the members of the blue team. He wanted to go and congratulate David, but decided against it. Wounds don't heel so quickly.

When Jerome, Terry and the boys got back to Albion Oaks that evening, it was time to pack for the journey home. They would have to leave Liverpool at midnight and drive to Holyhead to catch the Seacat at five am. David still wasn't talking to Luke. But his anger seemed to be melting. He did at least offer him a stick of chewing gum when they were cleaning muck off their boots outside the Mosely Park dressing rooms.

'Right, get that bedroom spic and span,' Jerome said.

He and Terry walked towards the front door. Luke, Tonka and David watched them closely. The same thing was on everyone's mind.

'I bet he knows,' Tonka said.

'Na, they wouldn't make the decision so quickly,' Luke replied.

David didn't offer an opinion. He simply pulled his sports bag from the boot of the car and walked towards the front door. At the same time, Stacy and Ringo were coming out for their evening stroll. David stood aside politely, taking a chance to shoot an envious glance at Luke.

'Off home?' Stacy said to no one in particular.

Tonka glanced at Luke scornfully. Just when things were getting back to normal, last night had come back to haunt him.

Tonka slung his bag over his shoulder. 'Yeah,' he said to Stacy. 'Take care.' Tonka walked towards the front door. Luke felt that uncomfortable feeling of guilt creep up his neck and constrict his breathing like an octopus tentacle.

Stacy wasn't bothered by the same problem. She wore a bright smile. 'How did it go?' she asked.

Luke leaned his arm on the roof of the car. He didn't know why. 'OK, I suppose. I'm not sure.'

Stacy didn't seem to be paying attention. She was more interested in Ringo who was running round her in circles, wrapping the leash around her shapely legs. She calmly unwound the tangle before looking up at Luke. 'Maybe I'll see you again,' she said softly.

They shared one last stare. Although Luke was desperate to turn away from the dazzling glaze of her eyes, he couldn't do it. In the end, she was merciful and broke her bewitching spell willingly.

Stacy walked off with Ringo trotting obediently by her side. Luke should have run straight into the house to quash the spurious rumours of his infidelity. But he just had to watch her go. Of course, at the same time he caressed his friendship bracelet and thought of Ella.

Seven hours after leaving Terry Culshaw's house in Liverpool, Jerome and the lads sat at the same table in Beefy Bill's Café waiting for their early morning fry-up. This would be a dubious meal to order on choppy waters. But the Seacat was half an hour from Dun Laoghaire harbour and the Irish Sea was as calm as a kiddie's paddling pool. Luke didn't want to ignite any suspicions Jerome may have about him and Stacy. Therefore he was determined to act as normal as possible. He sat beside Ella's Dad and discussed the trial while Tonka and David sat opposite, torturing him with icy stares and a dose of the silent treatment.

Luke was disgusted that they had stooped to such cowardly behaviour. It was bad enough women using this rotten tactic against him. But for men to use the same dirty trick against another man was outrageous.

'Do you know if we've made the second trial?' Luke asked, trying to get everyone's attention back on football.

Jerome was playing it cagey. He sipped his cup of tea casually. 'I know as much as you do,' he replied bluntly. He was lying. The lads could see it in his eyes. They were shifty and elusive. He knew more than he was letting on but seemed reluctant to spill the beans. A full-scale teenage interrogation was about to begin.

But Jerome pre-empted the hour of searching questions with a short, sharp press-release style statement. 'Look, the youth academy coaching staff will have a meeting with Alan Harper tomorrow. They'll make a final decision and Terry will be in touch.' He buried his face in a copy of Thursday's *Daily Mirror*, a measure designed purely to avoid eye contact. Luke, Tonka, and David looked at one another. They all shared the same fear. One of them had failed to make the grade. It sounded like Jerome wanted words in private.

The waitress arrived at their table and dumped four fry-up specials in front of them. Jerome was starving and tucked into his meal with great enthusiasm. The other three fry-ups remained virtually untouched.

Return of the Conquering Hero

Jerome dropped Luke off on Montague Avenue first. Tonka and David didn't bother to say goodbye. He watched the car disappear round the corner on to Harbour Road before carrying his bags to the front door. It was half eight in the morning.

The sun shot blinding rays of light on to Luke's back. It was a pleasant sensation that somehow relaxed his tired and aching bones. He sank his key into the front door lock and prepared himself for a hero's welcome.

Luke struggled up the staircase with his bags. When he reached the living room door at the end of the first floor landing he dumped them on to the floor. They crashed down with a loud thud. This was the signal. 'I'm home, come fuss over me.'

A minute passed by. There was still no sight or sound of Martina rushing to open the door. Luke could hear the lo-fi hum of the computer's hard-drive. He could even make out the gentle clitter-clatter of fingers punching keys. But the door would remain shut unless he fished out his key.

'Why am I surprised?' he said to himself quietly.

Luke opened the front door and walked inside. Martina popped her head out from behind the monitor. She smiled. 'Hi,' she said.

Luke couldn't believe it. Martina returned to her work with the minimum of fuss. The front door was wide open and he was standing in the living room with his bags by his ankles. Now, if he had just returned from a trip to Iceland for a pint of milk and a loaf of bread, Martina would be buzzing round him like an aggressive member of the paparazzi, firing question after useless question about his adventure. But, having spent two days on trial with a Premiership football club – and not just any Premiership club – two days on trial with Everton . . . and what does he come home to? 'Hi.'

Luke picked his bags up off the floor and stormed into his bedroom. He dumped the heavy black leather flight bag on his duvet and slung his sports bag along the floor. Then he ducked his head beneath the bed and clawed out his Mitre leather football. Luke walked back through the living room with the football tucked beneath his left armpit.

'Where are you going?' Martina said.

'Out,' Luke replied abruptly.

He slammed the living room door shut behind him and trampled down the staircase. Everything and everyone in his life had changed for the worse. The only thing left that made any sort of sense was football. Luke was in control when it came to football. So that's what he was going to do, play football.

The weed-ridden lawn in the back garden behind Mrs Hendy's house caught mounds of sunlight. Luke was there for two hours, kicking his ball against the wall. He practised passing with his weaker left foot and controlling a ball moving away from his body. Martina didn't bother to check on him before leaving for work. But Luke didn't care. He felt a thousand times better after two hours alone. A football and somewhere to kick it, that's all he needed. He stopped thinking about the stack of problems weighing his shoulders down; Martina, Ella, David, Stacy, Ronald . . .

Everything disappeared from his mind for two long, lovely hours. All Luke thought about was football. It was a breath of fresh air. But other people have a way of interrupting quality alone time.

'I thought you might be thirsty,' Mrs Hendy said. He spun round. She was standing on the edge of the lawn, holding two glasses of orange juice.

'At last,' Luke thought to himself, 'a friendly face.' He smiled and walked across to her. 'Thanks,' he said, taking a glass. Luke sank the orange juice in one go.

Mrs Hendy had been studying Luke's lonely kickabout carefully all morning. Over the past eighteen months she had grown accustomed to his varied range of facial expressions. She could tell when things were getting him down.

'Is something wrong, Luke?' Mrs Hendy asked kindly. Luke's head dipped. He flicked the football up on to his left foot and balanced it skilfully. Mrs Hendy waited patiently for him to raise his head.

'I'm just sick of them,' Luke said unhappily.

He allowed the ball to roll off his left foot on to the ground before smacking it firmly against the wall. Mrs Hendy had a fair idea of the identity of 'them', but she wanted Luke to tell her himself. She made a suggestion. 'It's a lovely day. How about a picnic?'

Luke raised his head again. He smiled at her. Mrs Hendy ushered him back into the kitchen to help prepare the picnic basket. Luke was happy to go along with her plan. He was sick of playing the villain.

The sun had been shining high in the sky all summer long. Perhaps clement weather books a three month stay in Ireland, one summer a decade. Luke couldn't remember the last time the sun had shone for six weeks uninterrupted. He decided to ask Mrs Hendy. 'When was the last good summer we had?' he said.

Luke's question caught Mrs Hendy unawares. She had been sitting on the old wooden bench, happily staring out at Dublin Bay from the top of Howth Head. She sat up straight and thought about it. 'I seem to recall a good run of weather in 1995,' she replied.

Luke nodded his head. His question and Mrs Hendy's answer had triggered a flood of memories. 'Oh yeah,' he said. Luke thought back to 1995. It was two years after Jay had left him and Martina for good. He was nine years of age and Everton had won the FA Cup that season, beating Man Utd in the final. It was Joe Royle's first season in charge. Martina was working at the Boots branch in Northside shopping centre and on the day of the final she agreed to wear an Everton scarf into work. Luke told her about a dream he'd had the night before the final. 'You have to wear it,' he pleaded. 'Everton won't win if you don't.'

Martina did it, despite a torrent of abuse from Man Utd fans all over the shopping centre. Suddenly Luke wanted that summer back again. He felt as though his mother had changed since then, maybe forever.

'Penny for them,' Mrs Hendy said.

Luke turned to face her. She was ready to listen, and he was ready to talk. But first he needed to stretch his legs. Luke stood up straight and walked forwards a few feet. He stared out at Dublin Bay and began to explain. 'None of them care, Mrs H,' he said. 'Ella, me ma, they couldn't care less.' Luke picked up a jagged splint of shale stone and flung it out over the cliff into the water below. It registered a distant clunk.

Mrs Hendy sat there quietly. She waited for Luke to turn and face her before she offered advice. 'Luke, what does football mean to you?' she asked.

He thought about it briefly before replying. 'Everything.'

Mrs Hendy invited Luke to sit down beside her by patting her hand on the bench. He did so. Mrs Hendy stared at him thoughtfully. 'A degree in Information Technology means the same to your mother as scoring the winning goal in a Cup Final for Everton means to you,' Mrs Hendy said. 'And a recording contract means the same to Ella,' she added.

Luke stared at his shoelaces. He had never thought of it that way before. Mrs Hendy placed her wrinkled right hand on top of his. She gripped it lovingly. 'Just because they're busy doesn't mean they don't care,' she said.

Luke thought about it. Mrs Hendy would never lie to him and her advice always made perfect sense. He lifted his head, looked into her sharp blues eyes and smiled. 'Thanks, Mrs H,' he said quietly.

Mrs Hendy didn't reply. Instead she reached into the straw picnic basket by her feet and picked out a bag of jumbo wine gums. They sat in the afternoon sunshine and stared out at Dublin Bay. Luke talked Mrs Hendy through the highlights of the two trial matches in Mosely Park. Afterwards he asked her to tell him more stories about her late husband Jimmy and her older brother, Charlie, who both fought as Spitfire pilots in the Battle of Britain during the Second World War.

When Luke and Mrs Hendy returned to Dun Laoghaire in the early evening, he was happily settled in a new frame of mind. He would drop Mrs Hendy back to Montague Avenue, then it was time to make things right with Martina, Tonka and David, and first of all, Ella. Luke crossed over from the top of Harbour Road to the bottom of Sycamore Street. He took a deep breath before entering Ella's front garden and put on his best apologetic face before ringing the doorbell.

Isaac answered the door. 'How's it going, our kid?' he said brightly.

'Good, Isaac, good,' Luke replied. 'Is she about?'

Isaac pointed over his shoulder to the kitchen door. This meant Ella was in her repair room. Luke felt rude leaving Isaac in the hall without a polite chat. He explained his hasty exit. 'I'm not being rude, Isaac, but I need to talk with Ella,' Luke said. Isaac knew the score. He gave Luke a helpful nudge down the hall. 'Later, bro,' he said. Isaac went back into the living room. Now Luke felt even better. His positive attitude and cheerful appearance was producing an identical response in people he came into contact with. He went out into the back garden and skipped down the path, confident things between himself and Ella would be back to normal in a matter of minutes.

Luke knocked on the door of the repair room.

'Who is it?' Ella asked.

'It's me,' Luke replied.

He could hear her groan. That wasn't a great start, but it was understandable considering the Output Studios incident on Monday evening. Ella opened the door but didn't invite Luke inside. She just blocked the doorway and stared him through. 'What?' she said bluntly.

Luke took one last deep breath to help him swallow his pride. He stared at her with his patented 'sorrowful puppy dog' look. It usually broke Ella's heart without him having to say a word. But not tonight. She remained stony. Luke realised a verbal apology would be necessary.

'Look, I'm sorry, OK?' he said.

Ella folded her arms across her chest. A plain, old 'I'm sorry' wouldn't be enough. Luke needed to come up with something better than that. He had no choice but to be sensitive. This was another sure-fire guaranteed way to melt Ella's heart. Telling her how he felt inside.

'I can't help feeling jealous,' Luke said.

Ella saw him as a confused, vulnerable little boy. Luke raised his head slowly; Ella bit her bottom lip. She was starting to crumble.

'Can we start again?' Luke said.

Ella seemed to nod her head in agreement. Luke moved forward slowly, edging closer to her. Tentatively he took hold of her right hand. Ella didn't object. Luke looked into her eyes, reading the signs carefully before gently moving forward to kiss her. It quickly developed into a full-blown make-up snog.

With victory secured, Luke broke off the passionate kiss. He held her in his arms, gazed into her dark brown eyes and delivered the winning line. The cherry on top of the icing, on top of the cake.

'I was wrong, you were wrong,' he said softly.

Ella's expression changed in an instant. She shoved Luke roughly in the chest, catching him off balance and knocking him on to the floor. Luke stared up at her in shock. Ella shook her head and gasped in disbelief. ' "I was wrong, you were wrong",' she yelled in a loud, clear voice.

'What?' Luke shouted back.

'I have done nothing wrong,' Ella said.

Luke climbed back on to his feet to continue the battle. The cheek of her; how could she claim to be completely innocent? It was time to spell out some home truths.

'You've got some cheek treating me like this,' he said.

Ella laughed at the dramatic snarl in his remark. 'Go away,' she said calmly. Ella turned away from Luke and went back inside her repair room. A manual for a Lexus mark III lay open on the table. She went to sit down, but Luke kept her standing with a rough tug on her left arm. He was determined to hammer his point home.

'I discovered you. If it wasn't for me you'd have nothing, no friends, no band, no life. You'd still be tucked in this poxy little shed with your car manuals.'

A slap to the face wouldn't do. Ella needed to express her anger with a more extreme measure of physical violence. She clenched her fist and landed a pinpoint right hook on to the bridge of Luke's nose. He could hear something crack. Blood spurted out.

'Get out,' Ella screamed.

Luke held his gushing nose. Ella seemed to be on the verge of tears. She was still furious with his crude outburst, but upset that she had hurt him so badly. There was a strange silence. Luke gave Ella a final piercing stare before he left the repair room.

On his way back into the kitchen, Luke bumped into Isaac. The thick pools of blood congealing on his blue Everton jersey said it all. He held his jersey to his busted nose, trying not to spill any red fluid on the kitchen lino or hall carpet. When Luke opened the front door, the Ford Probe was pulling into the driveway. Jerome and Mo climbed out of the car and stared at Luke in confusion. He quickly made his way outside the porch and tried to ghost by without a word.

'Luke,' Jerome said loudly.

Luke stopped outside the front garden and turned to face him. Asking the question 'what's going on?' seemed like a waste of breath to Jerome. Luke didn't know how to answer. But like most things in life, the solution was right under his nose. 'Give this to Ella,' he said. Luke ripped the friendship bracelet from his right wrist and placed it in Jerome's open palm. They stared at one another in a grim and gloomy silence. The broken, blood-stained friendship bracelet said it all. This break-up was serious.

'I have to go home,' Luke said.

He walked away from 18 Sycamore Street and crossed on to Harbour Road. He had tried to be understanding with Ella and failed miserably. Next on the list was Martina. But blood was thicker than water, Luke knew this for certain.

It was still bright outside when Luke reached Montague Avenue. Despite the downpour of blood that continued to flow from his nostrils, turning his royal blue Everton jersey a worrying shade of red, the pain had pulled into the background. It seemed Ella had failed to break his nose. Luke remembered hearing a loud crack when she landed her hammer blow, but that could have been her knuckles connecting with the bone. Of course, Luke was no doctor and could well be wrong. But on the journey from Sycamore Street to Montague Avenue, he was able to prod, pinch and probe the affected area without any pain or discomfort.

When Luke reached the front door, he realised he had forgotten his key. He reached for the gargoyle doorknob and rattled it three times. Twenty seconds later Mrs Hendy opened the door. A smile on her face quickly turned to a startled frown when she noticed his bloody nose. 'What happened?' she asked. Luke stepped past her into the hall. 'Ella,' he said quietly.

Mrs Hendy watched Luke climb the staircase. Although she didn't know the facts behind his bloody nose, she couldn't help but feel sorry for him. He cut a forlorn shadow against the white staircase wall.

Luke may have appeared downhearted. But inside he felt a funny sense of optimism. If Everton brought him back for a second trial, the chances were he would be staying with Terry

Culshaw again. The stains on his jersey were now symbolic. Each dark blotch of blood represented the shreds of guilt and doubt that had plagued him in Liverpool. But now Ella had made her feelings perfectly clear, Luke felt a sense of vindication. He could return to Liverpool and finish that kiss with Stacy. No guilt, no regret. All that mattered in the meantime was mending the broken bridges with his mother, Martina.

Luke opened the living room door and walked inside. Martina wasn't home. The computer was shut down and her bedroom door was wide open. Luke walked across to the fridge to search for a sheet of sticky yellow notepaper. Nothing. This was unlike Martina. She always left a note. Even if she was popping down to Mrs Hendy's parlour for a cup of tea she'd leave a note. Luke wasn't too concerned. There had to be a good reason for her absence. Something to do with work or her final exams.

To kill time Luke turned on the computer. While he waited for the machine to load Windows 95 he removed a frozen lasagne from the freezer and popped it in the microwave for ten minutes.

It was twenty past nine. Martina would be home in the next couple of hours. In the meantime, Luke would indulge himself with a game of Championship Manager 2. The last time he'd played was five months ago. Back then Martina had insisted he study hard for his Junior Cert exams and had given Luke a simple choice. Lose the Stretford Enders or CM2. This had been tough but fair. Luke had decided to keep real football and study for his exams on weekday evenings.

He loaded the game and chose to manage Everton under the name Alan Harper. He felt a giddy sense of happiness. Maybe things were changing, but there was no point crying about it. The best thing he could do was make things up with Martina, forget about Ella and look forward to seeing Stacy again.

ALONE IN THE WORLD

Luke fell asleep at the kitchen table sometime in the early hours of Saturday morning. Everton had a terrible first season in CM2 and narrowly avoided relegation. Luke had left the computer on through the night and the fan on the hard-drive was humming feebly. When he woke up it took him a few seconds to work out where he was. He turned round and noticed the microwave clock. Seven twenty-three am. Luke stood up from the chair. His back was as stiff as an ironing board. He attempted to stretch the aches and pains from his limbs by circling the living room. It was at this point a thought flashed in his mind. He glanced across at Martina's bedroom door, it remained ajar. She hadn't been home.

A sickening sense of panic wrapped Luke in a cold fear. An invisible force squeezed his lungs tighter and tighter, to the point where he couldn't find the energy to breathe. Immediately he jumped to the worst possible conclusion. He felt certain Martina was dead. Something terrible had happened to her.

Luke paced the living room nervously. He was on the verge of bursting into tears and the worst thing was, he had no idea what to do. Whom should he call? The police, a hospital, Mrs Hendy. What could he do? He ran into his bedroom and pulled on his tracksuit bottoms. He grabbed a pair of socks from the wardrobe and his trainers from beneath his bed. He ran back into the living room. Where was he going? He had no idea. But he felt a need to leave Montague Avenue, to find help.

Luke searched the kitchen top for his house keys. A car screeched to a halt outside. This wasn't something Luke normally got excited about. But now he scrambled forward to look down from the bay window. A navy, brand new Cherokee Jeep was parked outside the front door. A man and woman sat inside, kissing. Luke watched them for well over five minutes. He didn't blink his eyes once. When Martina finally climbed out of the passenger door and waved goodbye to Jonathan D'Argo, Luke had seen enough. The invisible force choking his lungs from inside his chest relented. He felt a deep sense of relief in the pit of his stomach, coupled with a swelling rage.

Luke sat down on the couch and prepared himself. He hushed his breathing and waited for the sounds. The front door opening, the gentle apologetic footfalls on the staircase. The creaky turn of the living room door lock. And there she stood, his mother, Martina.

They stared at one another, parent and child, except the traditional roles had been reversed.

'Hi,' she said nervously.

Luke closed his eyelids. He had been home for two days and Martina was now repeating the only thing she'd said to him since he'd got back. When he opened his eyes again she had moved across the living room to the fridge. She opened the door, took out a carton of orange juice and poured herself a glass.

Luke said nothing. He sat back on the couch, patiently waiting for an explanation, an apology, anything that could save a seed of respect for his mother.

'I should have called,' Martina said quietly.

Luke sat up straight. He stared at her with a calm, almost carefree expression.

'You are a selfish cow,' he said in slow and gentle voice.

Martina sighed feebly. She bowed her head and lifted her right hand to cover her eyes. She began to cry, tears streaming down her pretty face. Luke actually enjoyed seeing her this way. He got to his feet and walked towards his bedroom door.

'You've no right to say that,' she said sharply.

Luke came to an abrupt halt. He turned to face her. 'Always ring, or leave a note,' he said calmly.

This was a knockout blow. A quote straight out of Martina's code-book for responsibility. Words, phrases, sayings that she recycled any time he left in the house without her. These were rules and regulations he had been raised on. Luke knew this, Martina knew it. And there was no way to defend your actions when they ridiculed everything you believed in.

Luke pressed his right hand on his bedroom door handle. Martina was upset, but she wanted to work it out. She grabbed his arm and made him face her. 'Luke, I'm not just your mother, you know. I'm a person; I have needs,' she said weakly. Tears continued to roll down her cheeks. But Luke was unmoved. 'Don't I deserve a little happiness?' she pleaded.

Luke jerked his arm free from her hold. 'You make me sick,' he said in a soft and sinister tone.

Martina seemed to crumble. She broke down in an uncharacteristic sob. Luke didn't care. He carried on into his bedroom. It was clear to him now. This summer was his chance to transform from child to adult. Everton's youth academy would give him this opportunity. Surely he had done enough to secure a second trial. If, and when, Alan Harper called him back, Luke was determined to make it as a professional footballer. He would stand on his own two feet and move away from the hypocritical chains of friends and family holding him down.

Luke slept for the next twenty-nine hours. He had been running on empty ever since arriving home on Friday morning. A bloody nose and a night in front of a computer screen hadn't helped matters and it was early Sunday afternoon when his polar bear-like slumber was interrupted by a ringing telephone. It must have rung fifteen times before Luke stumbled out of his bedroom to answer it. The first four rings he thought were part of a dream.

'Hello,' Luke said with a gigantic yawn.

'Meet me at the sports store in an hour,' Jerome replied curtly.

The line was dead. Luke crawled back into his bedroom for an extra half-hour's snooze. He didn't know what time it was, but he trusted his brain to wake him up in time. When he finally made it up to Barnes Sports Store on Main Street, Jerome and Tonka were waiting impatiently inside. There was no sign of David.

'Right, one each,' Jerome said. He went behind the counter and opened the till. He reached beneath the plastic tray for coins and notes and pulled out tickets for the Seacat and InterCity. He handed them to Luke and Tonka. They looked at one another. David had failed to make the grade.

'The ferry leaves Friday morning, half ten. You walk on to Holyhead harbour, train station's right beside it. Terry will meet you in Lime Street. He'll fill you in on all the details.' Jerome stopped talking. He closed the till and placed his hands on the shop counter. He looked at Tonka, then Luke.

'Any questions?' he said.

There was one, but they already knew the answer. 'What about David?' Luke said softly.

Jerome shook his head sadly. But there was no time for sentiment. Life goes on. He moved down the counter to serve a customer who was waiting to buy Celtic's new home jersey.

Luke and Tonka stared at one another simultaneously.

They knew what had to be done.

The last time Luke and Tonka sat on the 46A together, they were on their way to Merrion Park to congratulate David. Now they were going to offer their condolences. When they arrived, David was standing in his front garden, kicking a football against the wall. He stopped and stared at Luke and Tonka. Things were still frosty between them. But Luke was determined to offer the hand of friendship.

'I'm sorry,' he said. He held out his hand. Despite a momentary stall, David was gracious and accepted the peace offering. Tonka suddenly felt the atmosphere change. No more piggy in the middle.

'Come on in,' David said.

Luke and Tonka followed him inside the front door. The Swaynes' house was empty. They sat in the front room watching MTV Select. Luke and Tonka were reluctant to ask questions, but David didn't seem too downhearted.

'When did you find out?' asked Tonka finally.

David lowered the volume on the TV. 'Yesterday morning. The boss called over,' he replied.

Now Luke and Tonka felt really uncomfortable. They both had their tickets for the Seacat and the InterCity with them. David spotted Luke's sticking out of his tracksuit pocket. He was going to ask, but when he saw the Stena Sealink logo he worked it out for himself. A bleak silence fell over the front room. The gloomy shadow of the first grey raincloud to appear in a month encroached on the front lawn. It was a deeply depressing moment. But Luke was still bursting with a sense of optimism and belief. More importantly, he knew how good a player David Swayne was. He had the character and the ability to bounce back from such a cruel body blow.

'It's not the end of the world,' Luke said. 'You were just unlucky.' Tonka backed him up. 'One bad game all season and it costs you a second trial. But that doesn't mean you're not good enough,' he said supportively.

Luke stared at David. 'You'll get another trial,' he said confidently.

David started to smile. He nodded his head in agreement. Suddenly, as if by magic, the gloomy silhouette blotting out the front lawn lifted to reveal a blinding ray of sunshine. It had to be an omen. The boys looked at one another. They started to laugh. When Luke and Tonka were leaving David's house he had the grace and dignity to wish them good luck with the next trial. Many people would say something like this to their friends, but inside, wish for them to fail. But not David Swayne, he had more class than that. One day it would show up as world-class. The next five days were strange for Luke. The only people he talked with were Tonka and Mrs Hendy. He did e-mail Ronald with the news of his second trial but that hardly counted as a conversation. As for Martina and Ella, avoiding any form of contact and the inevitable arguments that followed felt like a cumbersome weight lifting from his shoulders each morning. Luke had one major concern: impressing Alan Harper and earning a place at Everton's youth academy. What else was worth worrying about?

Trying Something New

Tonka and Luke travelled the distance from Dun Laoghaire harbour to Lime Street train station in near silence. Between Walkmans, books, magazines and light snoozes there wasn't much time for conversation.

Terry Culshaw made up for their six hours of comfortable silence with thirty minutes of frenzied conversation on the journey from Lime Street to Albion Oaks. Thankfully it was all to do with football matters.

'I must say, lads, you've done brilliant getting back for the second trial,' Terry said. 'The standard at Mosely Park was super. Best I've ever seen,' he added.

Tonka smiled, he felt geed up by Terry's compliment. After all, this man had played professional football for fifteen years. He had to know a thing or two about the standard required.

Luke was slightly more cautious. 'We're not there yet,' he said calmly.

Terry was impressed. He smiled at Luke in the rear view mirror. 'No, you're not. But you will be with that attitude,' he said positively.

Tonka felt even better now. But Luke had his mind on other matters. He noticed McPhersons, the local pub, passing them by in a flash. They were closing in on Albion Oaks. He prepared to move on with his life.

Luke and Tonka climbed the staircase to dump their luggage

in the guest bedroom. Terry and Rose were waiting in the kitchen below with orange juice, turkey, onion-and-cheese sandwiches and chunky Kit-Kats.

The sun blazed through the bedroom window. Tonka dumped his gear on the bed he occupied on the previous visit. Luke dropped his bags to the floor and stared out the bedroom window at the far-off bandstand in Albion Park.

'Hello again,' a familiar voice said. Luke turned round. Stacy stood on the landing, wearing a white bikini and a smile. Tonka nodded his head politely. But Luke wore a devious grin and a stare of obvious intent. 'It's good to be back,' he said confidently. Stacy actually blushed.

Tonka felt like a third wheel. He decided to make an exit. 'Are you coming downstairs?' he said.

Luke glanced at him. 'I'll be down in a minute,' he replied casually. Tonka nodded his head. It was none of his business how Luke behaved towards Ella or Stacy and he had no intention of becoming involved in any sordid little love triangle. He trotted down the staircase, leaving them to it.

Luke got to work quickly. 'Are you busy tomorrow night?' he said. Stacy was overwhelmed by his drastic change of mind. Ten days back he had fought her off with a stick. Now he was casually asking about her plans. She stalled in answering through sheer shock but eventually muttered, 'No, not at all.' Luke sauntered slowly from the bedroom on to the landing. He stopped two feet away from Stacy. The burning sense of attraction was like a current of electricity. He continued to stare into her wonderful emerald eyes. 'Would you like to see a film?' Luke asked softly. He felt no sense of guilt whatsoever. It was an uplifting experience.

Stacy on the other hand, wanted more information about his dramatic turnaround. 'What about Ella?' she said. Luke sighed sadly. He shrugged his shoulders. Stacy nodded her head and murmured, 'oh'. It took a brief moment of thought before her glum frown turned into a grin. 'It's really over?' she asked doubtfully. Luke nodded his head firmly. Stacy smiled. 'OK, I'd love to go out.'

Luke wanted to retain some level of hard to get. He broke off his stare and started down the staircase, leaving Stacy standing alone in the landing. 'We'll talk tomorrow,' he said. Stacy stuck her head over the banisters and watched him disappear towards the kitchen for afternoon tea. No boy had ever played her this way. It made Luke Farrell an intriguing prospect.

The next morning, Terry, Luke and Tonka left Albion Oaks at half eight. They were on their way to Bellefield for the first day of trials. It wouldn't be the same set-up as Mosely Park and Terry took each red traffic light along the way as an opportunity to explain. 'The second trial involves one hundred and fifty lads. The main difference with Mosely Park is the opposition.' The light turned green and Terry drove on. Luke and Tonka leaned forward from the back seat, desperate for more information. It finally came at the next red light. 'So, we break one hundred and fifty lads into groups of fifteen. And these groups play against our current academy players. The U-17 and U-19 teams.' Terry went on with more useless details; how many games in a five-day period, which member of the coaching staff would assess each match. Luke and Tonka didn't care. The startling prospect of facing an Everton team, albeit an U-17 youth side, set a blizzard of butterflies free in their stomachs.

'Lads . . . lads,' Terry said. He had been trying to raise their attention for a whole minute. Luke and Tonka finally focused on Terry. He smiled supportively. 'We're here,' he said. Terry climbed out of the car. Luke and Tonka sat in the back, afraid to move. They were in the car park of Bellefield. This was it. The time to make things happen. Tonka stared out one window; Luke stared out another. 'We can do this,' he said softly. They turned to face one another. Tonka didn't look too convinced, but Luke transmitted the abounding confidence and pure adrenaline flowing through his veins. 'Tonka, we can,' he said, reaffirming his belief. Suddenly, it all seemed possible.

Group One comprised players from England, Scotland, Ireland, Wales and even a kid from South Africa. It was a real cosmopolitan bunch. Luke and Tonka changed into a white Everton away strip from two seasons back and joined their team-mates on the touchline of the training pitch.

Everton's U-17 academy side stood in the centre-circle, wearing last season's blue strip. Alan Harper was running them through a team talk. They listened carefully and nodded their heads from time to time. Terry Culshaw was in charge of Group One. He clapped his hands together to attract the players' attention. They all surrounded him in a tight semicircle. 'OK, lads, listen up,' Terry said. 'No one's expecting miracles from you. Play it simple, work hard and compete.' It seemed simple enough.

Luke and Tonka took to the field and prepared for the kick-off. Just before the referee blew his whistle, Luke felt his knees buckle. Fear had struck at the worst possible time. Or so he thought. But five minutes later, Luke didn't have time to cough, let alone feel nervous. The pace of the game was frightening. The U-17s played Group One off the park. Their passing, their movement off the ball; it was like a fuzzy vision. By the end of the first half, the U-17s were winning by four goals to nil. Every Group One player was having a stinker. In fairness, with the exception of Luke and Tonka, this was the first time the players of Group One had played together as a team. The U-17s knew each other inside out and played accordingly. But Group One could make no excuses. They were gasping for air, fluffing simple passes and swiping mis-timed tackles. It was a shambles. Luke felt sure the second half would see a marked improvement. But the U-17s rolled on like a freight train. They scored five more goals and walked from the field of play like professional players. 9–0 was just a scoreline. Not a reason for rapturous celebration.

Luke spotted Tonka standing alone in the centre-circle, staring into space. He quietly edged up to the giant midfielder, a player who never looked out of place on a football pitch. But today he'd hardly won a tackle.

'What was that?' Luke said.

Tonka glanced at him. 'That was football,' he replied. 'We'd better get used to it.'

Tonka walked off towards the dressing rooms. Luke stood still and watched him leave. He noticed Terry waiting on the touchline to shake Tonka's hand. He didn't seem that upset with the result or the performance. Perhaps this kind of result wasn't so unusual for a first-day trial. Although it seemed naïve to do so, Luke felt confident about making the grade. If this was the pace of professional football, he would simply adapt. If Jerome Barnes and Terry Culshaw managed it, so would Luke Farrell and Tonka Matthews.

Moving On

Luke opted out of the conversation in the car on the way back to Albion Oaks. Terry and Tonka discussed Everton's future and former glories. It was interesting to hear the contrasting viewpoints of Toffees from different generations. Luke could have offered a few choice insights, but his mind was on other matters, or to be more precise, one other matter.

'What's the plan for tonight?' asked Tonka. He and Luke were unloading their sports bags from the boot of the car. Terry gave them the keys to lock up and was already inside the house.

'How do you mean?' Luke replied coyly. It was a question dripping with subliminal meaning. Scorching rays of sunlight pounded Luke's tanned arms and legs. Tonka stared at him, biding his time before offering a reply. He shut the boot door and locked up. 'Do you fancy a game of pool?' he said.

It was a clever ploy. He was giving Luke the chance to pull out of his date with Stacy. This absolved Tonka from guilt when the truth came out in Dun Laoghaire. He refused to become an accessory to Luke's betrayal. But as a friend, he was offering Luke a chance to change his mind.

'Erm, I kind of have plans,' Luke said.

Tonka shrugged his shoulders. 'Some other time,' he said casually. Tonka walked off to the front door with a clean and clear conscience. Luke had made the decision. It was his choice, and his alone. No one put pressure on him. Normally guilt would be eating away at him from the inside. But Luke had his eyes open. Ella was in the past; Stacy was the present and future.

Stacy was keen to keep her first date with Luke a low-key affair. During lunch, she sat beside him at the kitchen table and whispered the instructions in his left ear. 'Half seven, at the bandstand in Albion Park.' Terry and Rose didn't notice this covert communication. Tonka did, but he pretended to be more interested in hearing the recipe for Rose's vegetable lasagne.

When Luke came back from the bathroom early that evening, showered and scented for an evening on the town, Tonka sat on his bed reading a biography of Black Sabbath. He stared at Luke, feeling the need to comment. 'Are you sure about this?' Tonka said quietly, flicking a page in his book.

Luke sprayed some Lynx Alaska beneath his armpits before answering. 'Yeah,' he said bluntly.

Luke and Tonka debated the rights and wrongs of cheating on your girlfriend with a brief staring match. Tonka quickly conceded the point with an indifferent shrug of his shoulders. 'Fair enough,' he said softly. This was the last comment he would make on the subject. Luke respected this honourable manner. It never felt like Tonka was judging him or acting in that preachy overbearing big-brother way. If Tonka's personal opinion was 'this is wrong', he would say so, but always leave the final decision to Luke. If he wanted to cheat on Ella, that was his own business. Tonka obviously thought it wrong, but that was just an opinion. And anyway, he didn't know the full story. Luke spied the bottle of cK one on the bedside table.

'Tonka,' he said weakly.

'Go on,' Tonka replied with a sigh. Luke smiled. He reached over to the bedside table and picked up the bottle of cK one. He fired three conservative squirts on to his neck.

'Put a squirt in the palm of your hands and rub it on your earlobes,' Tonka said. Luke stared down at him. Tonka glanced up from page forty-three for a camera flash, a slender milli-second before turning his attention back on to the Black Sabbath story. 'It drives them wild,' he said without moving his lips.

Luke smiled. Tonka didn't approve of him cheating on Ella, but they were still friends. A small tip on grooming was a massive gesture. 'Nice one,' Luke said.

He squirted some cK one into his left palm and coated his earlobes. The digital clock on the stereo showed five past seven. Luke put on the old school sky-blue Adidas tracksuit top Ella bought him for Christmas and walked from the bedroom. 'See you later,' he said to Tonka.

Tonka didn't reply, but Luke accepted this as a lapse of concentration and not a deliberate snub. Terry and Rose were sitting on the couch in the living room watching Emmerdale. Luke stuck his head in to excuse his absence. 'I'm off out,' he said.

Terry muted the volume on the TV with the remote control. Rose looked at Luke with concern. 'Where are you going?' she asked.

Before Luke could open his mouth to try out the phony excuse supplied by Stacy, Terry cut in, '. . . Town with Stacy,' he said.

Luke was dangling in mid-air. He studied Terry's face carefully for signs of fury. Was he the kind of man who kept a loaded shotgun in his home?

'Do us a favour. Get a taxi home,' Terry said. He took a folded note from his shirt pocket and chucked it across the room. It landed on the floor, three feet from Luke. He stood still for a moment, afraid to move. He kept a close eye on Terry, but he didn't seem in the least bit vexed. In fact, he wore a friendly smile.

'Thanks,' Luke said. He bent down slowly to pick up the note but kept his eyes trained on Terry all the time, just in case this was a plan to catch him off guard. In fact, Luke was certain this trick was played on some greedy gangster in *Goodfellas* or *Donnie Brasco* who duly received a bullet in the skull.

'Be home by twelve.' Terry said.

Luke nodded his head.

'Have a good time,' Rose added with a cheerful smile.

Luke mumbled 'bye' and turned to leave. He was waiting patiently for a silent slug in the back. In the hall, outside the front door, on his way down Albion Oaks. Surely Terry would arrive with a lump hammer and a bag of nine-inch nails any time soon. But there was no sign. Still, Luke waited until he reached the bandstand in Albion Park to look at the note he had picked up from the living room floor. Ten pounds. Luke checked his watch. Quarter past seven. He felt certain Stacy would arrive late. In the meantime, he sat down on the top step of the bandstand. The sun continued to burn brightly in the early evening sky. Liverpool and Dublin seemed to be sharing summer, with the weather identically sublime.

'Hi,' Stacy said.

Luke followed her voice and turned to his left. She was standing on the lush green grass of the field below, smiling. She wore a matching white boob tube and long silk skirt, revealing just enough navel to send Luke's heartbeat racing.

Luke remained seated, and was in no rush to jump to his feet. He loved the view.

'Did Mum and Dad grill you?' she asked.

Luke stood up and wandered into the centre of the bandstand chuckling quietly. 'Very funny,' he replied.

In a moment of reckless abandon Luke decided to take a running leap from the centre of the bandstand on to the grass, six feet below. Stacy shrieked as he propelled himself through the air towards her. He landed cleanly on his feet, a few inches from her face and needed to press his hands against her shoulders to stop his momentum. They stared at one another blankly for a moment, but finally began to smile. Stacy slapped his arm playfully. 'That's not funny,' she said. They began to giggle. This was a picture book moment. Luke knew it; so did Stacy. Neither of them wanted it to end. But he had a feeling there were better moments to come.

'Where are we going?' he asked. Stacy slowly reduced her laughter to a seductive smile. She took Luke by the hand and led him across Albion Park. It was just as he thought, things could only get better.

Luke handed the Burger King cashier a ten pound note. He put one hand on the tray and held the other one out to pick up his change. 'Thanks,' he said to the glum-faced cashier. She wasn't wearing that happy Burger King corporation smile and it was easy to see why. Her face resembled a ripe tomato ready to explode and the skin on her neck seemed to blister beneath her itchy Burger King shirt collar. 'Next,' the cashier growled.

Luke picked up his tray and moved away from the counter. For a moment he considered returning to point out that the correct Burger King phrase was in fact, 'Can I take your order here, please.' But he was certain such a ribald remark would have earned him a strawberry milkshake in the face, and rightly so.

When he reached their table and placed the tray in front of Stacy, Luke shared his witty aside. Stacy's reply was typical of the evening so far. 'I'd remember that remark in case you end up working in a place like this.' Luke smiled. Their visit to the cinema had been a complete waste of time. Two hours in a dark room watching other people on a screen. This was a ritual most people depended on to break the awkward silence of a first date. Luke didn't need this break. He needed more time.

The bus journey into Liverpool city centre had been unreal. Their conversation had begun like most conversations do, with a mundane topic. The subject matter had drifted from the weather to music, to football, to whatever. It didn't matter what they talked about; Stacy had a way of explaining things. She could turn 'I bought a bag of Cheesy Wotsits on a wet Wednesday in March 1996' into an enthralling epic of Ben Hur proportions.

Luke gazed at her as she took a bite from her burger. It was close to eleven o'clock. They would have to head back to Albion Oaks soon. Luke wasn't mad about the idea. He would prefer to take a taxi to that place Mrs Hendy told him about, Gretna Green. Although it would probably cost him more than a tenner.

'I had a great time tonight,' Luke said.

Stacy stopped sucking on the straw of her Diet Coke. 'Are we going home?' she replied. This was a bizarre question. Luke was stumped for an answer or a suggestion. Stacy watched him carefully while taking another bite from her Whopper. The tension was unbearable. He just had to ask. 'What did you have in mind?'

Stacy dabbed the napkin against her supple lips. 'Wait and see,' she whispered softly.

Luke nodded his head.

'But could you do me a favour?' Stacy asked. It was a silly question.

'Name it,' Luke replied with a confident smile. His expression quickly changed. Stacy pushed a thin strip of black cloth on to the table and stared at him with those seductive green eyes. 'Put this on when I tell you to,' she said. Stacy balanced the plastic straw on the tip of her moist tongue. Luke's knees went again, twice in one day. He didn't say yes to her request. He just picked up the strip of black cloth and stowed it in the back pocket of his jeans.

Luke had no idea where they where. There was a taxi ride, but Stacy flagged down the cab and whispered the destination in the cabby's ear after tying the blindfold round Luke's head. There was a short walk, four beeps of an electronic keypad and the creaking of an iron gate. Luke was starting to get nervous. 'Stacy, where are we?' he asked.

'Not yet. Two more minutes,' she replied.

'Aowh!' Luke bumped his left shoulder into a stone pillar of some sort.

Stacy couldn't help but giggle. 'Sorry,' she said.

Whenever a girl blindfolds a boy, one unsettling thought runs riot through his mind. Practical joke, loss of clothing, embarrassing photos followed by blackmail. Luke didn't want to accuse Stacy of such a heinous crime, but this mystery trip was arousing his suspicions.

'Where are we going?' he said loudly.

'Shssh,' she replied.

Luke sighed dramatically but obeyed her order and kept quiet. There was an eerie silence surrounding them. Although they had entered a building of some sort through the creaky iron gate, Luke felt a chilly breeze blowing against his face and across his neck with each step he took forward.

'Are you ready?' Stacy asked. She had one hand on the knot of the blindfold and the other on his right shoulder. 'Welcome home,' she said softly.

Luke felt the black cloth disappear from his face in a flash. His eyes took a second to readjust to the darkness. But when he focused clearly, it was the most magnificent sight he had witnessed in his sixteen years on earth.

'Stacy,' Luke said weakly. He wandered from the brown dirt running track on to the hallowed green turf of Goodison Park. A bright blue blanket of stars hung overhead and a lone spotlight positioned on top of the main stand illuminated a small square of the pitch in front of the dug-outs. Luke twisted round slowly to take in all four ends of the ground: the goalposts, penalty areas, corner flags. An avalanche of names and faces flooded through his mind: Dixie Dean, Howard Kendall, Alan Ball, Peter Reid, Neville Southall, Kevin Sheedy. Toffee legends who stood where he was standing. It was the most majestic feeling. Something he could never hope to describe with words. Luke drifted like a drunken sailor into the centre-circle. Stacy walked after him, laughing with joy. 'Do you like it?' she said.

Luke slumped on to his knees. All power had drained from his legs. He looked up at her, desperate to wipe away the tears rolling down his cheeks but unable to raise enough power to his arm. Stacy kneeled down in front of him. She caressed his cheek with the palm of her right hand. 'I'd get used to this place. It's where you belong,' she said.

Stacy moved on to Luke, kissing him gently, caressing his chest and stomach with meticulous care. He moved his body to meet her halfway and ran his fingers up and down her long slender neck. For a while, time ceased to exist. Luke lay in the centre-circle with Stacy and forgot about Martina, Ella, Dun Laoghaire and all his problems. They simply paled into a void vacuum. Time became a myth and the universe consisted of three things: Luke, Stacy and Goodison Park.

Everything in Luke Farrell's life became clear and uncomplicated after the trip to Goodison Park with Stacy. Suddenly, the problems and hang-ups that kept his fingernails chewed to the bone and his eyes open in the early hours of the morning washed down the drain. Now there was no need to waste time worrying. Nothing was a problem, nothing was a hassle. Everything was a challenge accepted and a goal to achieve. In a matter of minutes, Luke had found that clarity of thought some people spend their whole lives chasing. Stacy Culshaw cultivated this change like a bee turning pollen to honey. Tonka watched this overnight transformation with great interest. He had spoken to Luke on four occasions since Saturday night. Each conversation was short, sweet and dealt solely with football matters.

Luke produced a hat-trick of stunning displays in the three trial matches after Saturday. In Group One's first match against Everton's U-19 team, he tore a highly-rated defence to shreds with incisive passing, wonderful close control and four inspired solo runs. The final score was 5–1 to Group One, with Luke scoring twice and setting up the three other goals.

Tonka had been holding his own in the trials. He had quickly come to terms with the pace and physical nature of the games but his performance was dwarfed by Luke's outstanding displays.

Thursday was the last game. Group One faced the U-19s in an eagerly anticipated rematch. Terry Culshaw felt the game was academic. Luke and Tonka would return for a final trial. Only Man Utd scoring a jammy goal in injury time was more of a certainty.

Five Days in Paradise

Terry Culshaw climbed the staircase to the first floor landing whistling the chorus of 'That's Entertainment'. It was half seven in the morning, time to wake the budding professional footballers from their slumber. He gave their bedroom door four firm knocks.

'Rise and shine, lads,' Terry said brightly.

Inside the bedroom, Tonka stirred at the sound of the fourth knock on the door. He half heard a voice mumbling 'rise and shine' and then the sound of heavy footsteps trotting back down the staircase. Tonka stretched and yawned. He glanced across the bedroom at Luke's bed. It was neatly made and empty.

'No surprises there then,' Tonka mumbled sleepily. He reached his hand up and yanked the curtains shut. There was still ten minutes snoozing time before he could seriously contemplate a trip to the bathroom.

Luke and Stacy had been up since five that morning. The final trial match was scheduled for eleven o'clock at Bellefield and straight afterwards Terry would drive Luke and Tonka to Lime Street station to catch the InterCity train to Holyhead.

This was their last chance to say goodbye and Luke had made a suggestion. They could watch the sun rise together. It was the perfect romantic gesture to end an amazing five days.

'I don't want to go home,' he said sadly.

He and Stacy were snuggled beneath a white woollen blanket at the steps of the bandstand in Albion Park. She leaned forward to kiss his cheek and then settled her head against his chest.

'You'll be back,' Stacy said confidently.

Luke relaxed. 'Yeah,' he replied.

It was a cocky statement. But it was the truth. In the last five days he had been playing football in a way he never thought possible. He was developing the subtle touch and understanding players like Cruyff, Maradona and Pele possessed. It was that skilful stroke of pure genius, making the extremely difficult look simple. Football had been broken down into simple lines. The confidence and self-belief needed to play such a flamboyant style of soccer had always eluded him. In fact, this confidence seemed to elude the majority of players. But Luke had it now. He was reading the game on that higher plane. Stacy had set free this ability.

He looked at her, asleep on his chest, her right hand clamped against the side of his ribcage. Luke needed to say it. This was the right moment.

'Stacy,' he whispered softly.

She opened her eyes and focused on his. He gently lifted her right hand from his ribcage and kissed the tip of her thumbnail. 'I think I'm falling in love with you,' he said shyly. Luke bowed his head with embarrassment. A few seconds later Stacy sat up straight and lifted his chin with her thumb. They looked into one another's eyes. Luke tried to speak but Stacy pressed his lips shut with the tip of her right index finger. She remained silent but slowly removed her index finger from his lips and kissed him passionately. It was a wonderful feeling to be back in love.

The journey to Bellefield was a boisterous affair. Tonka sat up front with Terry and argued each position of his all-time Everton XI. Luke sat in the back, half-listening to Tonka criticise the choice of Bob Latchford up front with Dixie Dean. He didn't offer an opinion.

They had been on the road less than fifteen minutes and already a horrible hole of unhappiness was boring it's way through his heart. To relieve the pain of her absence Luke pulled a set of passport photos from his tracksuit pocket. Stacy had taken him into John Moores University on Tuesday afternoon to check out the union bar. She'd suggested four wallet-size mementos from the passport photo booth. Luke wasn't keen at the time, but as always Stacy had managed to talk him into it. He couldn't imagine being without the photos now.

'Gary Lineker, my arse,' Terry said loudly. Luke tuned out of the argument again. All he wanted to think about was Stacy and Bellefield. These were the only things he cared about any more. Everything else in life and the world was meaningless.

Before the rematch between Group One and Everton's U-19s, Luke found himself feeling down. The thought of weeks or months away from Stacy was deeply depressing. But as soon as the referee blew the whistle for the game to begin, football conquered love.

Everton's U-19s had a point to prove and detailed two man markers to Luke. They followed him all over the pitch for the first twenty minutes of the match, snapping at his heels every time he got possession. Luke needed to shake them off to be an effective attacking force in the game. He had a quiet word with Tonka. 'Switch with me for a while,' he said.

Tonka nodded his head in agreement.

The two U-19 defenders looked to the touchline in confusion as Luke dropped deep into midfield. 'Go with him,' their coach yelled.

Luke knew this was a chance to shine. The Group One goalkeeper launched a kick from the edge of his area towards the centre-circle. With the ball still high in the air, Luke turned sharply and sprinted forwards. His marker spun in confusion, switching his attention from the ball to Luke. It was too late; the mistake had been made. Tonka controlled a flick on from a Group One midfielder forty yards from goal.

'Tonka,' Luke screamed, still sprinting forwards. He had covered sixty yards of the pitch in a matter of seconds and made a clever diagonal run in behind the U-19s' stagnant defence. Tonka acknowledged the call and lifted a neat lob over the top leaving Luke in a straight race with the on-rushing keeper who charged from his penalty area in an attempt to whack the ball clear.

Luke waited for the ball to bounce in front of him before swinging his leg wildly. The goalkeeper spread himself to block the shot, but Luke dummied the ball, allowing it to loop over the head of the fallen keeper. It left him with an open goal. He was still outside the penalty area and the two centre-halves tried to make up the ground with desperate sliding tackles. But Luke had time to slot the ball into the empty net. The eight people on the touchline clapped loudly.

'Good goal,' Terry said.

Luke glanced over at the touchline. Alan Harper stood beside Terry. He whispered something in his ear. Terry started laughing while Alan smiled. He jotted a quick note on his clipboard.

'You're home and dry,' Tonka said happily. He wrapped his arm round Luke's neck in an affectionate headlock. Luke smiled and patted Tonka on the back. 'You're not far behind me,' he replied.

They trotted back to the halfway line to restart the match. The morning sun was shining brightly overhead. It was the perfect reflection of their blossoming football careers.

Football at the highest level is rarely about fantasy. This was the shared belief that would play an important part in Luke and Tonka making the grade. After their dazzling piece of trickery, the rest of the match consisted of hard work; chasing the opposing midfielders, putting them under pressure, winning the ball back, using it wisely. These were the actions that won games. Especially between Group One and the U-19s.

The match ended 1–0, thanks in a large part to the tireless work of the midfield and defence of Group One. When the referee blew the final whistle, Luke and Tonka shook hands with the opposing players before heading for the dressing rooms. They had a train to catch.

'All the best lads, see you soon, please God,' Steven Murphy said. He was captain of the U-19s and had already signed a two-year pro contract with Everton. Luke, Tonka and the other lads from Group One returned the compliment. They were out of the shower room and changing back into their clothes.

'He's some player,' Tonka said.

Luke rubbed his hair dry with a brown towel. 'Yeah,' he replied unenthusiastically. They had been off the pitch less than ten minutes and already Stacy had wormed her way back into his thoughts. Tonka was well past caring. From what he could see, Stacy was nothing more than a brief infatuation. A holiday romance. Luke spent every minute in her company, but that wouldn't last for ever. He'd acted the same way with Ella last summer. 'Look how that ended,' Tonka muttered quietly to himself. He wasn't speaking as quietly as he thought. Luke overheard him and turned to face him innocently. 'What?' he said.

'Nothing,' Tonka replied. He puffed a sigh of relief.

Terry knocked on the dressing room door. He popped his head inside and addressed the lads as Group One. 'Thanks for everything lads. You've been a pleasure to work with. Expect a phone call in the next four days.'

That was that. The other boys began talking amongst themselves. Each player had a fair idea about his chances of a third trial. It was down to the individual and his performance over the four matches. Luke and Tonka stared at one another. Neither asked the question, but it was obvious. Have we done enough? Terry waited in the car park of Bellefield to drive them to Lime Street station. Luke and Tonka walked over to the car. Terry opened the boot and packed away their sports bags with the rest of their luggage.

Tonka nudged Luke in the ribs. 'Terry,' Luke said. Terry looked up at him. 'Thanks for having us,' he said. He walked over to the boot and unzipped his black leather flight bag. He lifted out a blue plastic bag which contained six cans of draft Guinness and a box of Milk Tray. Terry laughed as Luke handed him the bag. He picked out the box of chocolates.

'Cheers lads,' Terry said. 'Rose will be delighted,' he added.

Tonka and Luke climbed into the back seat of the car and waited for Terry.

'Milk Tray,' Terry muttered quietly, allowing himself a quiet chuckle. He sat behind the steering wheel and strapped in his seatbelt. Before he turned the key in the ignition he spun round to face Luke and Tonka in the back. He wore that same friendly smile. A genuine, welcoming smile that made him the perfect accommodation officer and an excellent youth team coach. 'Between you and me,' he said, 'You've both been invited back for the final trial next weekend.'

Luke and Tonka wanted to scream and shout with delight. But Terry tipped a finger against the side of his left nostril. This information was classified. They respected his appeal for decorum and made do with a simple handshake. The car pulled out of Bellefield. But it wouldn't be the last time they gazed at the lush green grounds. Suddenly all the hard work was paying off. Luke and Tonka were within touching distance of their dream.

SETTING PEOPLE STRAIGHT

Luke slept on the train journey to Holyhead. Tonka finished his Black Sabbath book. There was a comfortable sense of routine developing in the six-hour journeys from Liverpool to Dublin. It no longer felt like a long trek home, more of a transit to and from their place of work.

The sight of the Seacat moored at Holyhead harbour, waiting to whisk them across the tranquil Irish Sea had a friendly familiarity about it. The fantastic adventure of a football trial had long since disappeared. They were now firmly established on the road to fulfil their lifelong dream. The reality was a heartbeat away.

Luke sat in the TV lounge situated at the stern of the Seacat. It seemed like a single blink of his eye before Dun Laoghaire harbour flashed into view on the horizon. When Tonka returned from the toilet and started munching through his jumbo pack of popcorn, Luke made a quiet observation. 'Dun Laoghaire won't be home for much longer,' he said.

Tonka didn't stop munching his popcorn to offer an opinion. After a while Luke decided to follow up on his comment. 'Will you get homesick?' he asked.

'Stop jinxing it,' Tonka replied.

Luke smiled. It was a sensible reply and an excellent point. But he couldn't resist a sly dig at Tonka's caution. 'Chickens, counting, hatched,' he said sarcastically. Tonka wasn't interested. He positioned his headphones over his ears and clicked play on his Walkman. Luke laughed quietly. He turned his attention back to Dun Laoghaire, which drew closer and closer with each mechanical thrust forward. Despite Tonka's view to the contrary, he considered this trip home as nothing more than a chance to tie up loose ends.

All the houses on Montague Avenue were coated in a dark orange shade of late evening sunlight. Luke waved goodbye to Tonka who continued along the Avenue towards Harbour Road. The adrenaline which had carried him through the last five days was wearing thin. He felt a sudden craving for a four star pepperoni, a long hot bath and a night playing CM2.

'Luke,' Mrs Hendy said happily.

He was barely past the front door when she called him from the kitchen. But Luke was delighted to see her. He dumped his bags on the floor and jogged down the hall and through the kitchen door to meet her.

'Alright, Mrs H,' he replied. Luke gave her an affectionate hug. Mrs Hendy laughed, sensing a new Luke Farrell in the lines of his bright smile. She studied him carefully. 'I take it the trial went well,' she said.

Luke couldn't reply straight away. His thoughts turned to Stacy, Bellefield and Goodison Park under a midnight moon. Mrs Hendy's question had shot his depleted energy levels back up a little. 'Mrs H. That's the understatement of the year,' he replied.

After a brief exchange of pleasantries, Luke explained his travel fatigue to Mrs Hendy. He promised to call into the back parlour the next day for afternoon tea with an in-depth review of his trip to Liverpool.

Mrs Hendy was understanding. Luke apologised again

before heading upstairs. He put one last strain on his aching leg muscles and powered up the staircase in a flash. When he reached the living room door he heard two distinct voices inside. Martina had a visitor.

'Welcome home,' she said warmly.

Martina had the living room door open before Luke could get his key in the lock. He stood back in the landing, suspicious of this sudden bout of loving enthusiasm. It was an awkward stand-off.

'I'm so glad to see you,' she said quietly. Martina decided to go for broke and swooped forward, smothering her son on the landing with a desperate embrace. She applied the old bear hug routine. Luke would normally squeal and struggle to avoid such affection from Martina. But now he stood still, mindful of the false emotion and guilt-ridden desperation involved in her embrace.

'Hi,' Ella said. She had been hiding behind the living room door, patiently waiting her turn. Martina released Luke from her love-lock and scooped up his bags from the landing floor like any doting mother would do. 'I'll leave you to it,' she said.

Luke stared at his mother in disbelief. He felt as though he had walked on to the set of Dawson's Creek. Everything about Martina was superficial American pie, as if she were smiling at gunpoint. Ella seemed somewhat reserved. Luke sensed a genuine feeling of regret. She handed him a package prepared in royal blue wrapping paper. 'It's a peace offering,' she said softly.

Luke stared at her; she laughed nervously. He opened up the package. It was Everton's new white away jersey. Luke showed no emotion. He didn't feel any. 'Am I supposed to be happy now?' he asked bluntly. Ella was stumped. She knew making up with Luke was never easy. But her position was so weak, she was dreading the apology speech. It could run on for forty minutes. 'It's better if you let me talk,' Ella said.

Luke didn't reply. This was a clear signal to continue. Ella rubbed the back of her neck with the palm of her hand, trying to get the sentences straight in her head. 'I'm sorry about the cup final, the gig . . . well everything,' she started. 'I know I've been a total bitch recently. But music's important to me and Wesley has a real chance of getting us a record contract. Just 'cause I'm not around doesn't mean I don't love you.' Ella stopped dead. She was certain such an emotional plea would soften his stonewall expression.

Luke stood as stiff as a board. He stared at her like a suspicious bank clerk or a sceptical schoolteacher. 'Is that it?' he said coldly.

Ella sighed sadly. There was still some way to go in Luke's mind. She prepared her second line of apology. 'I don't fancy Wesley. He's just a friend.' Ella edged closer, she took hold of Luke's right hand and looked him in the eye. She was clearly on the verge of tears. 'I love you,' she said weakly.

Luke snapped his hand away with the speed of a scorpion flashing it's tail to sting. Ella was shocked by the force of his movement. She backed away a few steps. Luke watched her a while before deciding to follow.

'I want to show you something,' he said softly. Luke picked the passport photos from his tracksuit pocket and held them in front of Ella. She switched her stare from Luke to the images in the four snapshots. Ella crumbled right before his very eyes. She felt embarrassed and heartbroken. But Luke was unmoved by the tears streaming down her cheek.

'This is Stacy,' he said.

Ella gulped back the tears bravely. 'I know who it is,' she replied angrily.

Ella tried to leave, but Luke grabbed her by the arm and held her back. He was going to set things straight once and for all. Martina stood at his bedroom door. She watched in silence, afraid to interfere.

'You're nothing compared to her,' Luke started. Ella fought desperately hard to squirm free from his grasp. But Luke used his superior strength to readjust his grip and hold her in place. 'Weasel Adams can have you for all I care,' he shouted.

'Let me go,' Ella screamed.

'You're nothing compared to her.'

'LET GO !!'

'NOTHING.'

Ella strained forward to free her arm from Luke's vice-like grip. At first he fought to keep her in place, but when he saw she was clearly unbalanced, he released his grip without warning. Ella stumbled forward and took a heavy fall to the floor.

'Luke,' Martina yelled in shock.

There was a tense silence that seemed to last for hours. Luke stared at Ella who tried to pick herself up off the floor. He ignored his mother and hunched down to deliver the final blow. 'I never want to see you again,' he said.

Luke flung the Everton jersey at Ella's face. Martina wanted her to punch him in the nose again. But Ella just wanted to get away. She scrambled on to her feet and ran from the living room.

'Ella, wait,' Martina said loudly. She ran to the living room door but turned sharply and glared at Luke. It was a serious situation. But he felt complete vindication for his actions. Martina gave him a warning of things to come. 'Don't you dare leave this house till I get back,' she snarled.

Luke stood and stared confidently. Martina didn't like the thought of losing the stand-off. But she was determined to find Ella and apologise. 'You're dead,' she said before leaving.

Luke wasn't worried. He walked across to the living room door and shut it tight. His original plan sounded good. A four star pizza, a bath and a game of CM2.

BATTLE NUMBER TWO

Martina signalled her return to Montague Avenue with a thunderous clump of the living room door. Luke was unmoved and slid back in the bath, submerging his entire body beneath the water. A rapid succession of thumps against the bathroom door greeted his ears on his emergence from the soapy water.

'Luke,' Martina screamed. 'Open this door.'

There was a short silence followed by a demented succession of thumps. Martina was on the warpath and was determined to let him know.

'If you're not out of that bath in five minutes I'll break down this door,' she said loudly.

Luke wasn't impressed by her idle threat. He would soak himself until he and he alone felt ready to leave the soothing comforts of the water. Martina was preparing for war, but Luke wasn't concerned. He would defend himself against any attack with a sense of righteous pride.

Martina was waiting outside the bathroom door when Luke emerged with a towel wrapped around his waist. She wasted no time in lunging at him with a sharp slap of her hand across his face. It was to be expected and he took the impact of the blow with a calm expression.

'How dare you,' Martina yelled. 'How dare you treat another human being that way.'

Luke touched his roaring red cheek with his fingertips. He

walked into his bedroom to put on some clothes. Martina followed him, disgusted by his arrogant attitude. 'Did you hear me, Luke Farrell?' she asked.

Luke sat on his bed. He glanced up at her. 'Yeah, I heard you,' he replied calmly.

Martina watched him carefully. Luke opened the top drawer of a mahogany chest beneath the windowsill and picked out a plain white T-shirt, a pair of jeans, boxer shorts and socks.

'Is this a big joke to you?' Martina asked.

Luke pulled the T-shirt over his head. 'No,' he replied curtly.

Luke stood up and faced his mother. He had the boxer shorts and socks in his hands. He was silently demanding some privacy to dress. Martina wasn't moving.

'What's happening to you?' she said.

Luke began laughing. Martina didn't see what was so funny. But that didn't surprise him. The reason he remained so calm under the torrent of verbal and physical abuse was simple. He had no need to feel ashamed in the presence of a hypocrite. 'You have the cheek to act all high and mighty with me?' Luke said. 'You're a two-timing slut,' he added. It was an intense moment. Martina didn't scream or shout; she didn't break down in tears. But she had to stare at her son long and hard and then come to a drastic decision. Luke was well prepared to deal with whatever she could throw at him. After all, this was a flying visit to Dun Laoghaire. Albion Oaks and Bellefield would soon become his new home. Martina ended the staring match. She picked Luke's bags up from his bed and walked out into the living room. He watched her open the living room door and drop the bags on the landing outside. She walked back into the bedroom. 'Get dressed, then get out,' she said quietly.

Luke held his nerve and his tongue. This was a minor set-back; an incident to deal with and not worry about. Martina couldn't bring herself to look at him again. She left his bedroom and went inside her own. Luke dressed himself quickly and walked into the living room. He was starving hungry but decided to stay clear of the fridge. This was a test of character. A chance to move into manhood.

'So this is goodbye,' he said quietly as he opened the living room door. Luke didn't speak loud enough for Martina to hear, not that she would have replied. He pulled the living room door shut and started off down the landing to a new life. It should have been a frightening experience. But Luke actually felt a tinge of excitement flowing through his veins. There was no going back now. It was forwards or bust.

A Bed for the Night

Luke didn't have far to go for refuge. He took his bags and started on a short walk down Montague Avenue and up Harbour Road. Tonka had been asleep, but his father woke him up to hear Luke's story. They sat at the kitchen table with two cups of tea beneath the strip light which buzzed overhead.

'You can stay. But on one condition,' Tonka said.

Luke groaned. He knew full well what the condition would be, something to do with a hopeless reconciliation or heartfelt apology. He got up from the table and walked out of the kitchen. 'You can call her,' Luke said with a yawn.

Tonka watched Luke trample up the staircase. There was no point starting an argument. He was too tired for that. Instead, he walked down the hall and called Martina on the phone. He adopted his clear polite tone of voice which gave him an air of being a charming young man.

'He can stay tonight,' Tonka said.

'Thank you,' Martina replied.

The phone line went dead. Tonka was relieved but a little surprised. He had been expecting a lengthy interrogation. The secrets behind Luke's shocking transformation were hidden in Liverpool. Or so it would seem. This made him a crucial witness for the defence and a target for ruthless cross-examination. But Martina was in no mood to discuss the issue. It was a unanimous decision by all parties involved in

Thursday evening's fun and games that a good night's sleep was the best thing for everyone.

Luke and Tonka sat down for breakfast the next morning at half eleven. A good night's sleep had done little to lift the mood. A tense silence coupled with a fierce staring match was interrupted by the occasional sound of slurping or chewing. Luke broke the silence. 'What?' he said bluntly.

Tonka looked away. He didn't want to involve himself in a family dispute. He decided on a response. 'No comment,' he replied quietly.

Luke chewed his toast and muttered something under his breath. He could deal with everyone else offering him the cold shoulder. But Tonka would be on his way to Bellefield. They could be spending the next three or four years in each other's company. Tonka's respect mattered. 'Look. I've had it up to here with me ma and Ella. I don't want to know any more.' Luke said passionately.

Tonka looked at him. He sipped his tea thoughtfully but before he could reply there was a knock at the front door.

'Tell them I'm not in,' Luke said with a smile. Tonka wasn't amused. He went off to answer the front door while Luke sunk the butter knife into the tub of butter and coated another slice of toast.

'All right, Tonk.' Luke's heart stopped still when he heard that familiar booming voice. He jumped up from the table clutching the butter knife in his left hand. Tonka walked back into the kitchen, closely followed by Jerome. Luke calmed down. If Jerome was intent on breaking him into tiny pieces, he would already have the job done. But this was a friendly face, a calm presence trying to work out what had gone wrong.

'Can we talk?' Jerome said. Luke was still reluctant. But

Tonka set up the meeting by leaving the kitchen and shutting the door behind him. Jerome stood next to the door. Luke moved off into the opposite corner, putting as much distance between them as possible without moving into the back garden. Still, he had to gulp nervously; no witnesses.

'I just want to hear your side of the story,' Jerome said supportively. Luke thought about it briefly. Here was a new shoulder to cry on. Ronald's departure, D'Argo's arrival, Weasel Adams sniffing round. What was the point in taking a step backwards? These pointless gripes had ceased to matter. They were no longer problems. Luke had moved on.

He tried to explain this to Jerome. 'I dumped her. End of story,' he said callously.

Jerome's expression changed. 'That's no reason to push her over,' he replied.

'What about my nose?'

The situation had deteriorated dramatically. Jerome decided to cut straight to the heart of the matter. He put his hand on the kitchen door handle and prepared to leave. His parting shot was brutal. 'It's never your fault, is it? You've always got someone else to blame.'

Luke was outraged. 'What?' he said in a high-pitched shriek. Jerome walked down the hall and out the front door. Tonka stood in the middle of it all, watching in confusion while Luke stormed by and followed their manager into the front garden. 'Stuff you and your poxy team,' he shouted.

Jerome ignored him and climbed into his car. Luke wasn't giving up. He raced out on to Harbour Road and stood in front of the car. He banged his fist against the bonnet. 'You were nothing without me,' Luke said. 'You or your daughter.'

Tonka came out onto the street and attempted to pull Luke back inside the house. 'Get off me,' Luke screamed.

Somehow he manufactured superhuman strength to shrug Tonka off. Then he hammered his hand into the bonnet so hard he caused a large dent.

Jerome showed incredible restraint. He simply reversed the car back a few yards and pulled out on to the road. Luke was unrepentant, and still intent on shouting to the car as it moved off down Harbour Road. 'I don't need any of you,' he yelled. 'I'm going to make it, on my own.' Pedestrians walking along Harbour Road stopped briefly to watch his antics. He stared back at them aggressively, inviting complete strangers to have their say. 'Anyone else have an opinion?' he asked loudly. No one cared. Just another crazed teenage outburst, probably related to alcohol or drugs.

When he finally calmed down, Luke stepped back on to the pavement and noticed Tonka standing on his front doorstep. Not surprisingly, Luke's bags were sitting on the driveway. 'Well, what a big surprise,' Luke said sarcastically. Tonka slammed the front door shut. Luke began to laugh. This would be the cleanest break in history. But it didn't matter. He had the talent and ability to secure a life in Liverpool. When he shouted to Harbour Road about his intention to make it alone, he was telling the truth.

INDEPENDENCE DAY

The one positive thing about Luke's decision to alienate his friends and family when he did, was the weather. This was the perfect summer to be sleeping rough. Another scorching day of sunshine passed by as he wandered round Dalkey Quarry and Killiney beach killing time. Later that evening, he took what little money was left in his flight bag and bought food in a nearby Centra. Luke settled down beneath the shelter of the air safety beacon and tucked into his unconventional meal of barbecue Pringles and jumbo-size wine gums. It was half eleven at night and the stars were out in a sparkling show of force. In an effort to combat the affects of exposure, Luke was wearing a plain white T-shirt, an Everton jersey, Ronald's Dutch jersey and a navy fleece jumper beneath his Umbro rainjacket. Underneath his Levi's he had on three pairs of boxer shorts. Not that it was freezing cold, but the last time he slept in the quarry he had a sleeping bag. This time he had a white beach towel. Although Luke would be reluctant to say so, he was scared. Any unusual rustle in the bushes or whistle in the wind made him nervous. The neighbourhood that surrounded the quarry was inhabited by millionaire pop stars, actors and wealthy businessmen who built secluded palaces camouflaged by high white walls and tall pine trees. It didn't seem the sort of place where roving gangs congregated for drinking sessions. But Luke couldn't say for certain. He huddled in tight to the concrete wall of the beacon, closed his eyes and turned his thoughts to Stacy and Liverpool.

Suddenly, he heard the clear crisp sound of a twig snapping somewhere behind him. Luke sat up straight, his heart pounding at a tremendous rate. Now he could hear the sound of an empty can being squashed, then flung down a nearby concrete path. Footsteps were approaching. Luke held his breath and peeked his head out from the cover of the beacon to see who or what he was up against.

'David,' he said in disbelief. It was pitch black and he could be mistaken about the dark figure standing before him. But his initial reaction was that it was David Swayne.

'What are you doing here?' the voice replied. It was David all right. Luke blew an enormous sigh of relief and climbed to his feet. He walked up the grass verge to join him. They sat down on the opposite end of the safety beacon.

'You scared the shit out of me,' Luke said. He glanced at David. He was holding a clear glass bottle wrapped in a brown paper bag. He took a lengthy swig and offered a sip to Luke.

'What is it?' he asked.

'Vodka,' David replied casually. Luke shook his head. The last time he saw David was the day after the first trial. Tonka called for him before leaving for Liverpool the second time but his mother said he was out with Alan Giles and Copper Martin.

'Are you on your own?' Luke said.

'Yeah,' David replied blankly.

Only now was it striking him as strange; David wandering the quarry alone at midnight with a bottle of vodka. There was a blank, mechanical expression on his face and something sorrowful in his eyes. He stood up on the beacon and took another swig of vodka. Luke turned his head and watched David walk to the far end of the beacon. He decided to follow him. When he reached the edge he noticed David staring out at the moonlit Irish Sea. Killiney beach looked calm and peaceful below. The sea softly crashed against the shore.

'Have you been talking to Tonka?' Luke said. David didn't reply, yes or no. He kept staring out at the sea. Luke saw an opportunity to plead his case. 'I wouldn't believe a word he says. They've all got in for me. The boss, Ella, me ma . . .' Luke stopped to ponder the problem momentarily. ' . . . I think they're jealous,' he added sombrely.

David took another large swig from the vodka bottle. He was gulping the spirit back like water. Eventually he drank the contents dry. Luke watched anxiously as David flung the empty bottle high into the air. Its silent, majestic flight ended with a dull thud in the dense foliage below. He turned to face Luke with a menacing smile. 'You haven't got a clue, have you?' he said. Luke shrugged his shoulders. 'You actually believe you're hard done by,' he added.

'No, it's just . . .'

' . . . You've no idea what a real problem is,' David screamed loudly. It was that same expression on his face; identical to the one he wore in the Vortex. Luke was upset, he didn't feel the criticism was justified.

'Look, what do you know about my life?' Luke said proudly. 'I have problems coming out of me ears.'

David dropped his eyes to the concrete slabs beneath their feet. Luke had been prepared to talk at length about his vindication for treating people the way he did. But he caught a glimpse of the sadness in David's eyes. It was real despair; suddenly Luke's problems felt insignificant, although he wasn't sure why. A strong gust of wind blew across their shoulders. It rifled through the surrounding trees and bushes.

Luke was determined to keep David a friend, but only at a price. He offered a conditional olive branch. 'Look. I'm not saying I have it so hard. But I do have problems.'

It seemed like an hour before David raised his eyes from the ground to look at Luke. He stared at him with a strange sense of pity. 'Your life's a picnic,' he said sadly. Luke withdrew his olive branch. He was pumped full of all-out anger. He watched David stumble away, down the zigzag quarry path towards Killiney beach below. The light breeze was whipping itself into a timid gale.

'What do you know anyway?' Luke yelled. David wasn't listening, and at that moment, David Swayne represented the ear of the world and all the galaxies. 'Screw you,' Luke whispered. 'Screw the lot of you.'

Escape Plan

The rough but rhythmic racket of the Dart's wheels riding against the rails lulled Luke into a peaceful sleep. It was quarter past eight in the morning and sharp rays of sunlight flickered against the window. Luke fought hard to keep his eyes open, but this was the first sign of slumber since the InterCity train rolled into Holyhead train station two days earlier. He was exhausted. The night he spent beneath the air safety beacon with Tonka and David was far more enjoyable than last night. It was warmer for a start and he did manage at least a couple hours of sleep. Luke tried to look on his bout of insomnia as a growing-up experience. It was just another stepping-stone across the river to manhood and independence.

Early the next morning, Luke gathered his things together and headed for Killiney Dart station. The muscles in his neck and back were knotted and sore. His stomach rumbled and his eyes were full of dust and debris.

'Oh no,' he said. He let out a sleepy yawn. Predictably, he had fallen asleep and missed his station. The Dart was now pulling out of Lansdowne Road. It would take at least half an hour to get back to Dun Laoghaire. But this wasn't such a bad thing. It gave him a chance to sleep.

Luke had plenty of time to think things through on the train journey from Pearse Street to Dun Laoghaire. Nothing was set in stone and apologising was never out of the question. People change their minds all the time, fact of life. However, this was a comforting but irrelevant thought. He had no intention of apologising.

Montague Avenue somehow seemed different to Luke, who had been standing at the 46A bus stop for the best part of an hour, searching for a sign of life from the front door of No.8. Dun Laoghaire had been his home for nearly two years and yet he never felt a true sense of belonging. He was a northside boy, born and bred. His trip across the Liffey was always an extended visit, nothing more.

The green front door creaked open. Mrs Hendy appeared wearing her full-length camel hair coat. Luke picked up his bags and sprinted across the road.

'Mrs H,' he said loudly.

Luke had reached the concrete footsteps at the same time Mrs Hendy turned around to investigate his yell. She stared at him carefully. But before she could deliver her verdict on his recent behaviour, Luke interrupted. 'Please Mrs H,' he gasped. 'I just want to change my runners.'

Against her better judgement, Mrs Hendy stood aside and let him through the front door. She followed directly after and made a bee line for the telephone in the kitchen. She placed a call with the main office of Boots Chemists in the Bloomfield shopping centre. It was her hope that Martina could return home and resolve the conflict with a civilised conversation.

Unfortunately, Luke wouldn't be around that long. He was already inside the living room, retrieving the vital item from the special hiding place beneath the couch. It was a small blue bank book and the power to realise his escape plan.

Luke remained true to his word; he changed his trainers and scuttled down the staircase. Mrs Hendy blocked his path through the front door with her body and covered the lock with her right hand. She had a determined look in her eyes. 'It's not my place to interfere,' she said nobly. 'But in this instance, I feel an obligation.'

Luke remained calm. He was quite touched by her loving concern and said so. 'I appreciate it Mrs H. But you can't stop me. I'll go out into the back garden and over the wall.' Mrs Hendy tried to counter him with a firm verbal warning. But Luke stunned her silent with a loving kiss on the cheek. He smiled at her with a sincere affection that melted her heart. 'Thanks for everything. Thanks for being my friend,' he said softly.

It was a touching moment. But Luke knew what kind of a woman Mrs Hendy was; how determined she could be. If he wanted to escape he *would* have to climb the back garden wall. It didn't bother him. 'I'll send you a ticket for my first team debut at Goodison Park,' he promised. There was nothing more to say. Luke turned and raced down the hall, through the kitchen, and out into the back garden. Part two of his escape plan was a quick stop in the First Active on Main Street.

Watery lines of perspiration appeared in Luke's vision as he glanced up Main Street at the branch of the First Active on the corner. It was a punishing twenty-nine degrees with no refreshing breeze to combat the blistering effects of the midday sun. Everything in front of his eyes seemed to be melting, slowly dripping on to the crackling roads and pavements.

Luke absorbed a thick wodge of sweat from the back of his neck with the palm of his hand acting like a sponge or a damp cloth. He turned away from Main Street and focused on the Seacat. Foot passengers were beginning to board. He turned for one last glance at Dun Laoghaire. Now he was ready to leave. Luke slung his sports bag on to his back and picked his flight bag up from the boiling Tarmac ground. He climbed to the top of the gantry and handed his ticket to a tall, burly steward with a massive protruding chest and fine blond hair that could almost be classed as white.

'Have a pleasant trip,' said the steward politely.

'Thanks,' Luke replied. He took his ticket and walked on towards Beefy Bill's for a desperately needed fry-up. Already his mind drifted to future glory. In twenty years' time when he sat down to write the story of his football career, the steward would receive an honourable mention for his friendly phrase. Hopefully it would act as an uplifting marker to a dark and dismal chapter chronicling his brutal exile from former friends and forgotten family. A moment of quiet contemplation was interrupted by a female voice. A waitress asked Luke if he was ready to order. He pointed a finger at the full English breakfast on the menu. His journey to greatness was underway.

Making Your Way in the World

An old Motown song was running round Luke's head all the way from Dun Laoghaire to Lime Street. The words eluded him but the melody wouldn't go away. It began to drive him insane, trying to recall the song title from Jay's record collection. He couldn't figure it out, but somehow it seemed a fitting tune for a lone traveller.

The InterCity slouched to a grinding halt at platform two. Luke disembarked armed with eighty-six pounds, a bag of clothes, his football boots and his dreams. It wasn't such a scary situation. In a strange way, it was rather comforting. He was the only person with the ability to make a mess of things. And relying on his own resources (especially footballing) filled him with confidence.

Luke wandered into the stately marble plaza of Lime Street station. People zoomed by on all sides, travelling in fifteen different directions. There were echoey tannoy announcements, taxis parking and departing at the rank outside, trains screeching in and out of platforms and the thousand hectic sounds of a city. It made Luke smile. 'I'm an adult,' he said to himself proudly.

An anxious growl from his stomach ended his epiphany. He turned his attention to food and scanned the interior of the plaza. He counted three different newsagents, a Burger King and a small coffee bar. But then he noticed a bank of public telephones on a wall alongside the taxi rank. It crossed Luke's mind. A simple phone call. What would it hurt to let 'them' know he was safe and sound? But this moment of compassion quickly passed. That rush of hurt, anger and feeling of desertion. 'They' had waived their rights to his compassion with their attitude and actions over the last two months. That life was gone, for good.

Luke wandered across the palatial plaza floor to a staircase which led to the blue suburban line below. Stacy had shown him the route from Albion Oaks to Liverpool city centre the night of their first date. It was a simple case of catching a train travelling in the opposite direction.

Luke made several wrong turns in his quest to find Albion Oaks estate from the nearby train station. Eventually he took advantage of a chance sighting of McPhersons pub which he used as a landmark. It took five minutes to reach Terry Culshaw's front door. Terry was awaiting his arrival like an arch-villain in a James Bond movie casually stroking a pussy in the meeting room of his secret lair.

'What's your game?' he asked angrily. Luke shyly glanced up at Terry and Rose, who stood by his side. He sensed an ally in Rose. She wore an expression of pity and understanding for a confused teenage boy trying to run away from his problems.

Luke employed his 'on the verge of tears' eyes. Rose took it hook, line and sinker. 'Shut up, you,' she said, scolding Terry for his ill-mannered reception with a whack on the arm. Rose barged past her husband and slung her arm round Luke's shoulder. 'Come on, love. You must be starving,' she said gently. Rose and Luke walked into the hall. 'Terry, grab them bags,' Rose ordered.

Terry sighed in disgust. He waited in the hall for a

moment, determined to stamp his disapproval on her handling of the situation. But it was an exercise in futility. Terry would eventually have to bring in the bags. His only chance to assert some semblance of authority was to voice a warning. 'You're not eating a bite in this house until you ring home,' he said severely.

Rose and Luke were already in the kitchen. No one had heard his warning. Not that they would have paid any attention. Terry sighed and mumbled something under his breath, then he brought Luke's bags inside.

Dinner came first; the phone calls followed. Terry stood over Luke's shoulder in the hall while he dialled Jerome's number. It was something he'd rather not do, but life was about compromise. If Luke made the call he would be allowed to stay until the trial next weekend. If he didn't, Terry would send him home. It made little difference, Rose being on his side. Martina would get involved and that would be that. Luke made the phone calls.

Jerome didn't bother talking past 'hello' and 'put Terry on'. Martina was a different story. 'It's still engaged,' Luke said. Terry was sceptical. He looked at the phone number Jerome had given him and decided to dial himself. Luke smiled with a smug sense of vindication as Terry put the receiver back down. He stared at Luke carefully. 'You can ring in an hour,' he said. Luke nodded his head in agreement. 'Can I go for a walk in the meantime?' he asked.

Terry thought about it briefly. 'Don't be long,' he said. Luke was about to ask the question when Terry jumped in ahead of him. ' . . . She's down the park with Ringo.' It was an extremely awkward situation for both Terry and Luke. This whole mess couldn't be pinned to one single incident or action. It was a concoction of people, places, words, kisses and mistakes. 'It'll be dark soon. Make sure she's all right,' Terry said.

Luke felt a slight sense of acceptance. He watched Terry walk back inside the kitchen before turning and leaving through the front door. Maybe everyone wasn't against him. Albion Oaks could well become his new home, Terry his new mentor, and Stacy . . . Who knows? Luke sprinted from Albion Oaks in a blurry flash, desperate to reach Albion Park and Stacy as quickly as humanly possible.

Luke wasn't sure about the time. It was one thing that seemed to pass by at a strange pace when he travelled. The sun, moon, stars, daylight, dusk and dawn; these were the notches on the traveller's clock.

A pale blue sky illuminated by fading patches of scorched sunlight hung overhead. It reflected Luke's mood perfectly, exhausted but happy. Albion Park was deserted for the most part. A small group of teenage boys kicked a ball about on the football pitch in front of the bandstand. Luke stopped on the path behind the goalposts at the far end of the pitch. He searched each corner of the long rectangular grounds for Stacy. The sight of Ringo scampering out in front would be an early signal. She would saunter stylishly, ten feet behind, the red leather leash wrapped around her hand. Luke felt a giddy flush of excitement in the pit of his stomach. That dull sensation of emptiness she inspired had been clotted by the recent excitement in his life back home, but now it was returning.

A sudden spherical flash of white before his eyes broke his attention. 'Yeah,' a voice said. Luke glanced at the lads standing by the goalpost, waiting for him to fetch their ball. He turned, jogged across the path into the clump of tall oak trees that lined the grounds of Albion Park and chipped it back. 'Nice one,' one of the lads said.

Luke was unable to acknowledge the compliment. He had located Stacy. She was standing in the centre of the bandstand, embracing a tall black kid. From their actions they seemed to be more than platonic friends. It was hard to believe; yet another betrayal. Luke watched the intimate actions for an uninterrupted three minutes. Then a frantic panting broke the spell. He glanced at his feet. Ringo was scratching at his leg, desperate for some kind of human attention. Luke bent down and rubbed the puppy's neck, ears and belly. He turned his attention back to Stacy in the bandstand and waited for that sensation of boiling hatred and betrayal to overwhelm him. But it wasn't coming. Luke had become immune. He had mastered the first important lesson to learn on the path to adulthood. Betrayal is a normal state of affairs. People cheat, people lie and people do bad things to you. It's a fact of life, something you learn to accept, something you learn to live with. Luke was finally learning.

'Come on, Ringo,' he said warmly. Luke picked up a long slender stick from the ground and flung it back across the field towards the bandstand. Ringo scampered after it. Luke took cover behind the bough of an oak tree and waited patiently. Stacy and her mystery man had noticed the stick in the air and Ringo chasing after it. They were now looking into the trees to check the source of the chuck. Luke stepped out of the shadows. He stared at Stacy briefly, but his expression was calm and collected. Her mystery man was confused, another innocent party in her manipulative three-way affair. But this wasn't The Jerry Springer Show. No need to kick it out of one another.

'You're welcome, mate,' Luke said quietly. Stacy didn't shout out his name. But she watched Luke closely as he walked from Albion Park. It was a tricky situation, but something she was sure she could handle.

'Who's he?' Mystery man asked. 'Oh, no one,' Stacy replied with an automatic sense of cunning.

Luke rang Martina when he got back to Albion Oaks. Terry and Rose stood in the hall and watched the extremely curt exchange. Then Luke handed the phone over and allowed Terry to explain things to Martina. He was representing Everton FC and the image of the youth academy. Teenage boys running away from home and travelling hundreds of miles alone to play in trial matches wasn't a great reflection on the club. It was his job to defend their professionalism. But Terry was also a fellow parent and talked to Martina with empathy and understanding. A few minutes later Rose took over, she was a mother and made a personal guarantee of Luke's well being.

During all this, Stacy and Ringo came through the front door. Stacy stared at Luke. 'Can we talk?' she asked quietly. Luke followed her and Ringo into the kitchen, leaving Terry and Rose to say goodbye to Martina. Stacy opened the kitchen door and ushered Ringo out to his kennel. When she closed the door, she tried to explain. 'Look, it's not what you think,' she said.

Luke smiled. 'Save it, Stacy,' he replied calmly. 'We had a laugh, you've moved on. End of story.' They stared at one another in silence.

'You're not upset?' she asked tentatively.

Luke shrugged his shoulders. 'We had a great five days. Let's leave it at that.' There was an uncanny sense of serenity in Luke's face. He was talking sincerely; he really didn't care. 'Friends?' Luke said. He stretched out his hand. Stacy stared at the symbolic gesture of friendship suspiciously. What little game was he playing?

Eventually she shook his hand, trying to inject all her

alluring sexuality into her touch. It didn't work, Luke removed his hand and smiled. 'I'm in a heap. I'm going to bed,' he said.

'Night,' Stacy replied softly. She watched him walk from the kitchen with an anxious feeling of desire pounding blood from her heart at an appalling pace. A boy who wouldn't walk across a road of barbed wire, broken glass and scorching hot coals for her company and her kiss. There could be nothing more attractive in a man.

GETTING ACQUAINTED WITH DUNCAN

A week can pass by in what seems like seconds when you have your mind on more important matters. Luke didn't think about Stacy, Martina, Ella, or anyone else who had caused him upset in the last two months.

Football occupied every waking moment. And in his dreams, long and arduous campaigns would end with victory at places like Wembley, the Olympic Stadium in Rome, the Nou Camp, Goodison Park (of course) and on one strange occasion at Craven Cottage.

An away fixture against newly-promoted Fulham was the setting for Everton's eleventh league title. Goals from Campbell, Ferguson and youth team superstar Luke Farrell sealed a famous 3–1 win and wrestled the title from Man Utd's grasp by a single point. Each morning, Luke would replay the highlights of his slumber visions while completing a five mile jog to Bellefield. Then he would empty from his backpack the morning snack lovingly prepared by Stacy and watch the figures that dominated the landscape of his dreams.

'Fergie, Fergie,' called captain Stephan Hughes. Luke watched from the touchline as Francis Jeffers held off the advances of Michael Ball to slide a perfectly weighted through ball into the path of the marauding midfielder who then slammed a vicious shot past Paul Gerrard. 'Yessss,' Pembridge shouted, celebrating extravagantly to raise a response from his team-mates in blue bibs.

Luke smiled as Pembridge jumped on to the back of David Weir, the Scottish centre-half who almost stopped his shot with a despairing, last ditch tackle. It was hard to hear the joke. But the rest of the first team squad joined in the banter. Luke didn't strain too hard to listen. He was more than content to watch quietly from the side-lines.

Walter Smith, the manager, called his players into a huddle. Training was coming to a close. Hughes had scored the winner, hence the celebration. Now the serious stuff took place. Luke finished off his bottle of Lucozade Sport. It was day five of first team pre-season training and Luke had watched each session diligently. Most of the time the players were running, pounding their bodies into shape with ruthless exercise. Brief games of football had taken place yesterday and today. Luke watched both kickabouts, concentrating his attention on Duncan Ferguson; his movement, positioning, running off the ball and most importantly, his finishing. He felt he was learning a great deal.

Walter Smith dismissed his troops for the day. Luke was standing a good thirty yards from the entrance to the dressing room, watching his heroes disappear inside from afar. But he felt privileged just to be in their presence. Duncan Ferguson and Michael Ball were the last players to reach the entrance. They walked side by side. Luke almost fainted when Michael Ball pointed his way. They were looking over at him. Although Terry had cleared it with the management for Luke to watch pre-season training, he suddenly felt like a trespasser.

'Here, kid,' Duncan Ferguson said loudly. Luke pointed his finger at his chest weakly. Duncan Ferguson nodded his head. 'Catch,' he yelled.

It travelled upwards like a soaring ballerina, then down like a shooting star. Luke caught it. Duncan Ferguson stared at him and smiled before disappearing inside. Luke examined the treasure. A plastic bottle for holding Lucozade Sport. It was three-quarters full with the orange liquid and had the letters E.F.C imprinted on the side. He smiled proudly. Endorsement from his hero and the greatest omen of all time. 'Me and you, Duncan. Me and you,' Luke said happily.

Luke couldn't remember a single detail of his journey from Bellefield to Albion Oaks that day. He made it back alive, that was a miracle in itself. The forty-five seconds of his life when Duncan Ferguson engaged him in conversation had a numbing effect similar to local anaesthetic. It was five to five when he reached the front door. Waiting there for him was the perfect sight to knock him back into the realm of reality. Tonka. Luke made no attempt to be gracious. He headed straight inside.

'Luke,' Terry said angrily. Luke knew better than to ignore Terry, who had been more than accommodating to Luke's situation. He turned round to face him. 'Now, I know certain things have happened between you two. But once you're inside my house or Bellefield training ground you will be expected to show the proper respect. Is that clear?' Luke didn't want to reply first. He stared at Tonka who held a similar silence.

'Is that clear?' Terry said calmly.

'Yeah,' Luke replied.

'Yeah,' Tonka added.

Terry nodded his head. 'Good,' he said.

It was a tactical truce. Tonka and Luke both knew this. It was unfortunate considering how much time they could be spending together over the next three or four years. But Luke was becoming an adult. He could deal with tricky situations in a mature manner. Tonka took his bags from the boot of the car and shut it before walking up to the front door. He and Luke exchanged sulky stares before Tonka asked, 'How's your new girlfriend?'

Luke replied in kind. 'Piss off.'

Silence reigned between the two for the rest of the evening. It wasn't a difficult state to maintain even though Tonka and Luke had to share a bedroom. They both fell asleep before midnight. The next morning they would decide their futures on the football pitch.

Bellefield was empty and silent when Terry and the boys arrived. It was quarter to nine in the morning and the trial match was scheduled to start at ten. Terry shut off the car's engine and turned to explain their early arrival. Tonka and Luke stared at him in silence. 'You and nine other boys are in competition for three places at the academy,' Terry said sombrely. This was the painful part of his job. It was now when the pain of rejection would sting the worst. 'All the best,' Terry said softly.

Luke and Tonka stepped out of the car and walked from the car park to the touchline of the main pitch. They glanced around the empty training ground and saw all their dreams and nightmares balanced on a knife edge. Luke had been confident all week. He still felt sure of gaining a place at the youth academy but he realised others might fail. He glanced at Tonka sympathetically. 'Good luck,' Luke said quietly. Tonka stared at him. 'You too,' he replied sincerely. They shook hands before walking off to the dressing rooms together, much like Duncan Ferguson and Michael Ball. It was crunch time, and Luke planned to deliver.

At ten o'clock Luke, Tonka and nine other players wearing the new Everton home kit lined up against the U-19s who were wearing an old yellow and blue away strip. It seemed ironic that the eleven lads combining together as a 'team' were actually the ones in competition. Luke had never seen any of his team-mates before. They had each come through the two sets of trials without crossing paths. Now they were expected to form a team. The referee blew his whistle and Luke tipped off with a tall red-headed striker. The ball went back to Tonka who hit an anxious pass forward. It ran through to the U-19s' goalkeeper.

Luke glanced at Tonka, then at the touchline where Alan Harper and his team of four coaches took notes. 'Not the greatest start in the world,' Luke thought to himself. But he quickly dispelled any pity for Tonka from his mind. He had no wish to be cruel or callous, but there was a goal kick to face, Alan Harper to impress and schoolboy forms to be won. Over the course of the first twenty minutes, the high standard of play became apparent. Luke had played against the U-19s twice before, but this time they were a different proposition. They tackled like tigers, closing down every opposing player in possession as if he had an open shot on goal. The improvement in their play was logical. Anyone picked to join the academy would be in direct competition with them. This was obviously a 'welcome to the club' occasion.

Luke responded to this hectic pace and settled in. Drifting right and left, he found gaps between the midfield and along the back four and started to work his magic. The red-headed striker was the first player to benefit. Luke picked up an incisive pass from Tonka wide right and cut inside. He was moving across the edge of the penalty area when the left-full put a desperate tackle in. Luke waited for this swipe before turning back outside. He had a split second to look up and noticed the red-head unmarked at the back post. Luke chipped the ball over a line of heads. It landed perfectly for the red-head, but somehow he managed to miss an open goal from three yards. 'Jesus,' Luke said in disgust. It didn't matter to him. He had done all he could, by putting it on a plate, and would have made a positive impression on Alan Harper. As for Red-head, surely he had blown his chance of a contract.

The match wore on. The U-19s took a two-*goal lead before half-time and coasted through the remainder of the game. A host of players in blue turned in mediocre displays. Everyone apart from the goalkeeper, who produced a string of top-class saves; Tonka, who won countless tackles and headers, passed the ball neatly and covered every blade of grass on the pitch; and Luke of course, who cut open the U-19s defence time and time again.

Only the heroics of their goalkeeper kept the score to zero. But Luke had a plan to remedy the situation. With a mere minute remaining, Tonka knocked a superb ball up to the red-head on the edge of the penalty area. He won the header and knocked it back into Luke's path. It was the perfect time to be clever. The No.5 ran out to block Luke, who shaped as if he were going to hit it on the volley. It was a trick. Luke poked the ball through the No.5's legs, rounded him and charged into the penalty area. The No.4 closed off his path to goal, waiting for Luke's next move.

With a perfect piece of trickery, Luke played a one-two against the No.4's left shin. It ricocheted back into his path and left the No.4 frozen to the spot in shock. Although the No.6 and No.3 tried to toe-poke the ball to safety, Luke had just enough time to smash the ball high into the net, past the goalkeeper.

Luke was up-ended by the No.3, his sliding tackle arriving after the ball was gone. He lay on the ground, staring up at the bright blue sky. 'Sorry mate,' the No.3 said. Luke didn't reply but he was far from bothered. He had just sealed his place at Everton's youth academy with a dazzling piece of skill; the kind of football everyone wants to watch. Alan Harper, Super Toffees around the world, everyone.

WAITING TO EXHALE

Alan Harper asked four boys to stay behind after the match was over. Luke and Tonka were included in the group of four. The other boys who were asked to remain in the corridor outside Alan Harper's office were the goalkeeper, Kevin Lewis, and the red-headed striker, Thomas Horne.

The maths didn't add up. Three places on offer and four players asked to stay behind. Someone would be returning home with their dream in tatters. The office door swung open. 'Kevin,' Alan Harper said.

Luke, Tonka and Thomas watched Kevin walk across the corridor and enter the office. Surely the first boy called inside would be offered forms. The three lads glanced at one another anxiously. The last boy called to the office; that was the straw to avoid.

Four minutes later, when Kevin came back into the corridor, he wore a calm grin. Alan Harper stood behind him. 'Thomas,' he said.

Kevin Lewis didn't say anything to the lads. He ran down the corridor, probably to phone home and pass on the good news to his family and friends. Luke didn't have such concerns.

Thomas went inside the office. A surprise candidate for a position at the youth academy, but Luke had only seen him play today. He could have done enough to seal his place in the first and second round of trials.

They both wanted to avoid it. But eventually their eyes

locked on the same path. Luke and Tonka stared at one another sadly. This was it, Russian roulette. The next name called by Alan Harper would go on to live the dream, at the expense of his best friend.

'All the best,' Tonka said warmly.

Luke wasn't sure for a second. But he could see it in Tonka's eyes. This was a sincere slogan. The problem being, Luke didn't feel the same way. 'You too,' he replied feebly. Luke looked away. He was ashamed by his blatant greed. But this was the most important moment of his life. Everton, football, it was his life. Tonka was a good friend, but friendship was dwarfed by the chance of a glittering career in professional football.

The office door creaked open. Thomas Horne appeared from the blinding sunlight, smiling happily. Alan Harper threw a long shadow on the floor of the corridor. He was holding a loaded gun, ready to take aim and shoot the bullet. 'Luke,' he said, almost in slow motion.

Everything stood still. Freeze-frame. He had won his place at the youth academy. Tonka Matthews had come so near and yet so far, but this was the one clichéd idiom that summed up life and football perfectly. When you shoot on goal, it either goes in, or stays out, there is no inbetween.

Thomas Horne wandered down the corridor in an obvious daze. Luke and Tonka stared at one another. It was a tense moment, but Tonka dispersed his obvious disappointment with a gallant smile. Before Luke turned to enter the office, Tonka held his thumb aloft. It was a noble gesture, one which Luke would never forget. But a gesture he could never have made if the tables were turned.

'Take a seat,' Alan Harper said.

Luke obeyed his order and waited patiently for Alan to

climb into his chair behind his thick oak desk. He shuffled about until he found a comfortable position then stared at Luke with a pleasant smile.

'First off, I think you're an excellent player and a great prospect,' Alan said. 'However, I can't offer you a place at the youth academy,' he added bluntly.

Luke sat there, unable to fathom what had just been said. Alan Harper had three sheets of white paper in front of him. He tapped the bottom edges against his desk, folded them neatly in half and handed them to Luke.

'Let me explain,' Alan said quietly. 'We're on a very tight budget here. I can sign three kids from anywhere in the world for the academy and fourteen local lads for the centre of excellence. Unfortunately for you, the academy is stocked up with strikers and attacking midfielders. What I'm looking for this year are goalkeepers, defenders, and defensive midfielders.'

It was still to sink in. Alan Harper's explanation made little sense. Thomas Horne was a bundling striker; why was he offered forms? Luke felt weak. Soon he would have to stand up, shake hands and walk from the office. He wasn't sure he could make it up on to his feet.

'But, as I said before, I think you're an excellent prospect,' Alan said. 'That's why I'm giving you these contact numbers.'

Luke turned his fuzzy focus on to the white sheets. He opened up the first page and noticed the crest of Preston North End, then Crewe Alexandra and Wigan Athletic. Alan Harper explained. 'Any lad that makes it this far with a Premiership side will more than likely be offered forms at a lower league club. This is a list of our local affiliates.'

Alan Harper reached across the table. He squeezed Luke's arm, grabbing his immediate attention. 'Prove me wrong, kid. Five years from now I want to see Walter Smith paying four million quid to bring you back here. I really do.'

It was a second chance of sorts. But Luke couldn't see it that way. All he could see was the failure. The humiliation of crawling home to Dun Laoghaire with his tail firmly between his legs. Alan Harper shook his hand. He showed him out of his office, where Tonka sat waiting for bad news.

Luke's face was a deathly shade of white. Tonka didn't know what to think and Luke didn't know what to say. In the end, they passed one another in total silence. While Tonka was invited inside Alan Harper's office to fulfil his life-long dream, Luke stumbled outside to consider a way to rebuild the ruins of his life.

Terry met Luke outside the dressing rooms. He refused to be downhearted and bombarded Luke with a list of great players who went on to greatness after initial rejection. David Platt, Ian Wright, Peter Beardsley, Kevin Phillips, even Kevin Sheedy was let go by Liverpool only to go on and become an all-time great Super Toffee.

Terry was upbeat about Luke's chances of a place at Preston North End. 'It's a good set-up there. The reserve team coach is a mate of mine. I'll have a word,' Terry said.

Luke didn't reply. He was sitting on the steps outside the dressing room. His head was bowed low, level with his kneecaps. Terry, who was standing opposite him, bent down and slapped his face gently. It caught Luke's immediate attention.

'Listen to me. This isn't the end. This is just a set-back,' Terry said.

Luke stared at him. He nodded his head and tried to be positive. But Terry's attention had been drawn to something behind Luke. 'Congratulations,' he said.

'Thanks,' Tonka replied quietly.

Terry stood up. He looked at the two lads and decided to

make an exit. 'I'll be over at the car when you're ready,' he said.

Tonka sat down beside Luke on the steps while Terry walked over to the car park. It was a tricky situation for both of them. But Tonka was determined to follow Terry's example and focus on the positives. He took the white sheets from Luke's hands. 'I'm not being a smart-arse. But I think you should go on these trials. You're bound to get in somewhere,' Tonka said. 'And think about it. If you join Wigan Athletic, you'll have a much better chance of getting first-team football there than I will here.'

Luke still felt like someone had removed all his internal organs through his mouth. But the words of kindness and logical optimism were beginning to soothe the pain. 'Yeah,' he replied sparingly. Luke got to his feet and forced himself to smile at Tonka. He stuck out his right hand. 'Congratulations,' he said bravely.

Tonka stared at his outstretched hand for a while. A simple handshake wouldn't be enough in this case. He got to his feet and applied a loving bear hug. Luke had no qualms about this show of affection. He wrapped his arms round Tonka as best he could and squeezed as much comfort as possible from his massive shoulders. Bellefield training ground was empty by now, except for Alan Harper, the odd cleaner, Terry Culshaw and two best friends embracing.

THE LONG ROAD HOME

Tonka remained in Liverpool to finalise the details of his place at the youth academy. He managed to hide his overriding excitement and joy in Luke's presence. Again, Luke wasn't so sure he would have acted the same way if the roles had been reversed.

Terry, Rose and Stacy drove Luke to Lime Street station to make sure he got off safely. Ever since Alan Harper broke the news, Terry had been leading a campaign to keep Luke's spirits as high as possible. He was a football man; he had been in the professional game twenty-three years as player and coach. He had witnessed and experienced all the highs, lows and heartbreaks the game had to offer.

'I rang Michael Turner this morning. He's the reserve team coach at Preston North End,' Terry said at the station. 'He's offering you a two-week trial in November,' he added. Terry handed Luke a letter with the details. 'If you want to go over, give him a call next week,' he said.

Luke smiled at Terry. It was a nice gesture and he appreciated it. He held out his hand. 'Thanks for everything,' Luke said.

Terry nodded his head slightly. 'All the best, kid.'

Rose Culshaw couldn't resist the temptation to give Luke a loving hug. She whispered in his ear, insisting he keep his chin up and prove Alan Harper wrong. The Culshaws were like a political party, preaching a philosophy of persistence.

Finally Luke waved goodbye and walked to the ticket office at platform three. The ticket collector clipped his stub and waved him on. Luke was almost at the door of the first carriage when he heard a voice scream his name. 'Luke.'

He turned round. Stacy, who had been extremely quiet since hearing the news of his failure at Bellefield, was standing at the ticket office. Luke walked back to meet her. 'I need your address,' she said.

Luke stared at her, noticing a different look on her face. It wasn't the usual look of confidence or calm sophistication. It was an eager, anxious, almost panic-stricken expression. Stacy had a pen and small notepad at the ready.

'What do you need my address for?' Luke asked. It was a good question. As far as he could tell, he and Stacy were water, long since passed under the bridge. There was nothing more to say or do, especially in light of his recent failure.

'I thought we could write to one another,' she said shyly. 'Maybe we can meet up when you're here in November.'

Luke thought about the sheer lunacy of her suggestion and the erratic nature of her actions over the last two months. There was no thread or logical order to her behaviour. To his mind, Stacy was just another feminine creature. Irrational.

'Maybe we will,' he replied coldly.

Stacy watched Luke walk back to the first carriage of the InterCity train and disappear inside. She was in a state of rolling desire. Luke was now well aware of Stacy's character. Boys who wanted her were boring; boys who remained aloof became desirable in the worst way possible.

In any normal set of circumstances, unearthing such an insight would be a reason for celebration, but Luke was finding it hard enough to raise the enthusiasm to keep breathing in and out.

The Seacat seemed to slide across the still waves smoothly, moving closer and closer to Dun Laoghaire harbour. Luke sat in a half-empty TV lounge holding the piece of paper Terry had given him at Lime Street. It had Preston North End's crest emblazoned across the top. The last three hours of his journey had been one long battle to look on the bright side of life. He had a golden opportunity, a second chance to breathe new life into his dream. But this is where the problem would arise, time and time again, no matter what way he spun the tale to suit. The dream was to play for Everton, not just to play professional football with any old club.

Then there was Dun Laoghaire. A place he'd waved goodbye to for the final time nine days ago. He was returning, to eat a piled plate of humble pie. It was a meal he had no appetite for . . .

'Docking in fifteen minutes,' a distorted voice announced over the tannoy. Luke decided to leave the TV lounge. He gathered together his bags and walked out into the corridor. Somehow, the closer they came to Dun Laoghaire, the harder he found it to breathe. A dizzy sensation overcame Luke in the corridor; it blurred his vision. He needed fresh air or water.

A men's toilet was up the corridor on his left. He stumbled inside. It was a shock to the system. An awful rush of nausea flooded his body. Luke vomited into a white marble sink, retching his guts dry with four throaty hurls. The sickening stench of the spew forced him backwards. He fell into a vacant cubicle and slumped on to the toilet seat. Luke began to cry uncontrollably. A confluence of emotion had come to a head. The vile gases of anger, fear, frustration and regret spewed forth in a wave of vomit. These noxious ingredients had been building up on the lining of his stomach ever since Martina and Ella failed to show for the Cup Final. But with every opportunity to vent these vile particles from his system, Luke would sigh and bury them in the pit of his stomach. They would eventually explode. They had exploded. Luke sat in the cubicle and sobbed until the Seacat docked in Dun Laoghaire harbour.

It was raining heavily when Luke disembarked the Seacat at Dun Laoghaire harbour. Night-time, a cold, gusty wind and torrential rain. What a perfect setting to return home.

He moved down Montague Avenue with his eyes trained on the cracked pavement below. Every few seconds he took a deep breath, storing up air for his apology. Tonka was still in Liverpool, there was no chance of a bed for the night on Harbour Road, so apologising to Martina had become a necessity.

He only noticed the blue light when it flashed across the pavement in front of him. Luke lifted his head. An ambulance was outside 8 Montague Avenue. The front door was open and neighbours had already gathered by their own doorsteps to witness the event.

Martina appeared from the front door clutching a crumpled tissue in her right hand. Her face looked pale and empty. She stood to the far side of the concrete steps to allow a paramedic through the door. He carried the tail end of a stretcher. There was a body on board, covered with a blood-red blanket. The paramedics carried the stretcher down the steps carefully and loaded it into the ambulance.

Luke watched in silence, heavy droplets of rain pelting on to his face, a fierce wind driving tiny pellets of dust and dirt into his eyes. Martina spotted him standing there. They stared at one another a while. 'Surely not,' he said to her silently. Martina's eyes fell to the ground, signalling a sombre 'yes'. Luke turned his attention back to the ambulance. The driver pushed the metal handle upwards, locking the back door. He made his way along the side of the ambulance. Martina stood in front of Luke and blocked his view. 'Luke,' she said softly. Martina wrapped her arms around his shoulders and began to cry.

Luke kept his eyes on the ambulance. It pulled away from Montague Avenue with a mute siren. He had a million questions to ask. When, how, why? But they could all wait till later. Luke had one job now. He helped his mother inside No.8 and locked the front door behind them. Mrs Hendy would never see him play at Goodison Park.

THE FUNERAL

Sarah Josephine Hendy was seventy-nine years of age when she died. The coroner concluded that she had suffered a massive heart-attack sometime on Saturday morning. At the same time Alan Harper told Luke that his footballing future lay away from Everton, Mrs Hendy had gone to meet her maker.

The funeral took place on Thursday morning. Martina had been prepared to organise things but an elderly man called into 8 Montague Avenue on Sunday morning. His name was Martin Butler, executor of Mrs Hendy's will. She proved to be as sensible and conscientious a woman in death as she had been in life.

Money and instructions had been left for Mr Butler to execute when she passed away. All Martina and Luke had to do was turn up at St Christopher's chapel in Dun Laoghaire and follow on to Deansgrange Cemetery.

For the first time that summer, the skies opened wide and rain poured down for five days on the trot. On Thursday morning Luke dressed in his black Levi's cords and a black polo-neck jumper Martina had bought specially for the occasion.

They went to the chapel and sat through the service. A small congregation of elderly men and women listened as the minister talked about Sarah Hendy's bravery in fighting for what she believed in, whether it be love or freedom. Martina clutched Jonathan D'Argo's arm as tears streamed down her cheek. She was genuinely upset. But Luke couldn't manage a single tear. He had cried when Everton turned him down, but the death of his special friend seemed unreal. He found it hard to recall the details of her face. Maybe it had all been a dream. Mrs Hendy, Dun Laoghaire, Ella, the Stretford Enders, perhaps it was all an illusion. The minister asked the congregation to rise and sing Hymn 236. Mrs Hendy had specially requested this hymn. Luke listened to the words, trying to uncover a hidden meaning.

It continued to rain heavily at the cemetery. The minister kept it short and sweet and the small congregation soon passed on. Luke, Martina and Jonathan were all that remained by the side of the grave.

'Are you ready?' Martina asked quietly.

She wrapped her arm round Luke's left shoulder lovingly and stared into his eyes. He turned his attention back to the gaping hole in the ground. 'I'll follow you on,' he replied.

Martina didn't want to leave him there alone. But she sensed a need for him to say a private goodbye. Jonathan squeezed Martina's shoulder and quietly urged her to leave. She took his outstretched hand and prepared to walk away.

'Er, Luke,' Jonathan said nervously.

Luke slowly turned to face him. He watched as D'Argo dug his hand into his trouser pocket and pulled out a crisp ten pound note. He handed it to Luke. 'Get a taxi home,' he said.

There was something conceited in his offer. But Luke did sense a shred of sincerity. Perhaps he needed to give Jonathan D'Argo a chance to prove himself. After all, they were all mature adults.

'Thanks,' Luke said, taking the ten pound note.

He watched Martina and D'Argo walk off towards the cemetery car park. Before he turned his attention back to the grave, he spotted two familiar faces standing by the flower stall. Jerome and Ella were buying flowers.

Luke kept his eye on Ella until she noticed him. She and Jerome stood still for a second, beneath the cover of a red and white striped golfing umbrella.

Luke turned his attention back to the grave. Mrs Hendy was their friend too. They deserved the opportunity to say goodbye. 'I'll be back, Mrs H,' Luke said to the gaping hole. He tucked his hands into his jacket pocket and walked off towards the exit at the opposite end of the cemetery. Ella and Jerome watched him leave.

'Come on, babe,' Jerome said.

He and Ella walked up to the grave to pay their final respects. But already she was thinking of following Luke. It didn't take a brain surgeon to figure out where he would go. That information belonged to ex-girlfriends.

Luke spent Jonathan's ten pound wisely. First he went into Centra in Blackrock and bought a 500ml bottle of Coke and eight packets of Jonnie Onion Rings. Then he invested in a return Dart ticket to Howth. Finally he put 30p in the public phone box and dialled home.

'Hello, Ma?' Luke said.

'Luke, where are you?' Martina replied.

'David's house. I'll be back later.'

There was a moment of silent uncertainty. Martina had the feeling Luke was lying, but she didn't know why.

'OK,' she said. 'Be careful.'

Luke put the phone down and checked the electronic timetable. The next Dart would be leaving for Howth in seven minutes. Plenty of time to tuck into a packet of onion rings.

When the Dart pulled into Howth train station, Luke had just polished off the last packet of onion rings. He slugged the drains of his bottle of Coke and threw the litter into the plastic Centra bag.

It was still a miserable day. The torrential rain had subsided to a steady drizzle but the wretched breeze had whipped into an icy gale more becoming of mid-January. Luke started off through Howth village, on his way to the summit. He was still waiting for tears to flow.

Mrs Hendy was gone. This was a tragedy, and yet no tears. Everton failed to offer him a place at the youth academy. A trivial matter and Luke ends up a sobbing wreck. It was an outrageous injustice. But he felt no sense of guilt for his reaction. Perhaps the correct emotions had been mixed up in his mind.

The top of Howth Head was deserted, save for an old man wearing a navy sailor's cap and a red raincoat walking a golden Labrador along the nature trail. Luke sat down on the same wooden bench where he and Mrs Hendy had sat three weeks before. He caught a clear glimpse of Dun Laoghaire across the bay. All his problems were lying in wait. A tiny speck on the landscape.

'I'm sorry, Mrs H,' Luke mumbled softly.

He bowed his head and began to sob.

Luke could not be certain how long he sat there crying. Twenty minutes, an hour, he just wasn't sure. With such a majestic view on offer, it seemed wasteful to bow your head at your feet. But Luke could barely raise the strength to cry, let alone look out at Dublin Bay.

Out of the silence, Luke noticed footsteps behind him. They drew closer and closer until they suddenly stopped. Someone was standing behind him. He didn't bother to turn his head and check. A few seconds later, something dropped from the sky above on to the wooden bench.

It was a tattered friendship bracelet. Luke spun round slowly. Ella stood behind him. 'You forgot this,' she said with tears in her eyes.

Luke was hesitant, but eventually drew the courage to lift the bracelet up from the bench. He held it between his thumb and forefinger and studied it carefully. The breeze blew strands of hair across his face.

'I'm so sorry,' Ella said.

Luke turned and glanced up at her. He didn't feel he deserved it, but she was offering him a second chance. For a moment, he was determined to refuse her offer on the grounds he was a dickhead. But he could see it in Ella's eyes. She didn't care about Stacy. She was still in love with him. In a way, that's all he ever needed to know.

Luke got to his feet and hugged Ella. He tried not to, but he started to cry again.

'I'm sorry,' he repeated time and time again.

'So am I,' Ella replied in refrain an equal amount of times.

Keeping a Promise

Luke and Ella had a busy day on Sunday. The Stretford Enders had pre-season training in Woodlawn Comprehensive in the afternoon and Martina and Jonathan promised to take them out for dinner in the evening. But before all that, there was the small matter of Mrs Hendy.

Luke stood at the graveside, clutching Ella's hand tightly. The sun had reappeared after its week-long holiday and shone brightly on the black marble headstone. Sunday was a busy day in the cemetery and dozens of mourners were laying flowers at the final resting place of their loved ones.

'I brought you these,' Luke said softly.

He placed a freshly-cut bunch of white carnations from her own back garden on the grave. He arranged them neatly, and stood back to inspect his work. A sudden shot of sadness hit him in the heart. He sobbed quietly. 'I'm really sorry Mrs H, I wish I'd had the chance to say goodbye.' The wind whistled behind his ears. 'The trial didn't go too well. Everton turned me down,' he said sadly. Luke's head slumped in a forlorn fashion. But then he found courage and strength from a loving squeeze on his palm. He stared at Ella, confident of her love. For the first time in months, he was secure and happy. 'But I'm going back,' Luke said positively. 'I've got a trial with Preston North End. They're not as big a club as Everton, but I'll just start in a lower league and work my way up.'

The utter silence of the grave reminded Luke how much

he would miss Mrs Hendy. Her sensible words of wisdom, her stories about Charlie, Jimmy and the war, tea and cream cake in the back parlour. That was all gone, forever. A single tear streamed down the right side of Luke's cheek. But he kept smiling. 'I'm still gonna make it, Mrs H. I'm gonna play at Goodison Park for Everton,' Luke said confidently. He paused briefly. 'And when I do, I'll score my first goal for you.'

Luke turned to Ella. It was time to go. They walked from Deansgrange cemetery together. Along the way to Sycamore Street, Ella explained how Weasel had sent off the demo tape of the Funky Starfish to Sony Music and attracted the interest of their chief A&R man in Ireland. They were playing a showcase gig in the Temple Bar Music Centre next Wednesday.

'Will you put my name on the guest list?' Luke asked dryly.

'We'll see,' Ella replied. 'Only if you're good.'